cl
F
FLOR

[AUG 2 3 2011

The Days of the King

Books by Filip Florian

Little Fingers

The Băiuţ Alley Lads
(coauthor with Matei Florian)

The Days of the King

The Days
of the King

FILIP FLORIAN

Translated from the Romanian by Alistair Ian Blyth

HOUGHTON MIFFLIN HARCOURT
BOSTON · NEW YORK
2011

Library of Congress Cataloging-in-Publication Data
Florian, Filip.
[Zilele regelui. English]
The days of the king / Filip Florian ; translated from
the Romanian by Alistair Ian Blyth.
p. cm.
ISBN 978-0-547-38835-9
1. Dentists—Fiction. 2. Friendship—Fiction. 3. Kings and rulers—Fiction.
4. Illegitimate children. 5. Bucharest (Romania)—History—19th
century—Fiction. I. Blyth, Alistair Ian. II. Title.
PC840.416.L64Z5513 2011
859'.335—dc22   2010049821

Book design by Linda Lockowitz

Printed in the United States of America
DOC 10 9 8 7 6 5 4 3 2 1

F
FLOR

Gift -ES
8-11-11
2200

To Luca, my son,
who knows what joy is

Contents

The Days of the King

1 ✤ Farewell

THE FAREWELL EVENING in Berlin concluded just as it ought to have concluded: with the scrawny body of the dentist sprawled across the bed, his head buried in that moist, gigantic breast whose mate had long ago been sliced off by the saber of a drunken hussar. Previously, he had drained six mugs of beer, bought a drink for anyone who entered the tavern, clinked glasses, hugged friends and strangers (what a commotion!), and won one last round of whist, to the cheers of the kibitzers, mainly because his fellow card players had connived to make him emerge triumphant, not cheating in broad daylight but by the light of the candles on the tables and shelves. He departed from Der Große Bär after nightfall, letting them think that he would quickly return from the latrine and order another round for one and all; in any case, he left his coat on the back of his chair, a scuffed overcoat, rather short in the sleeves, that had not found a place in his luggage for Bukarest and now eased his exit from the scene. Later, at the brothel, they welcomed him with whoops and tears, in the way whores do when they take an occasion to heart. The establishment did not shut up shop in his honor, it is true, but the girls were able to bid their farewells one by one, plundering minutes from other customers and lavishing on him slices of time as sweet and filling as slices of cake. It was a night on the house. Fräulein Helga even cracked open some champagne, and in her capacity as madam she kissed him on the brow and gripped him by his fly, begging him to forget their teeth, but remember their tits. In Rosa's room, as she was oiling her skin with an infusion of jasmine (with her right hand), now and then stroking her bottom (with her left), the girls entered one by one and allowed him to take a leisurely leave. He nibbled a plump earlobe, with its stud of blood-red glass imitating ruby, hidden beneath chestnut locks; with his lips he circled a pair of rounded knees; he ran the tip of his tongue along the spine of a lean and milky back, having first sprinkled it with cinnamon; he bit two fleshy buttocks; and he slowly breathed warm air over a rosy belly until he found its button and desired to swallow it. His fingers, like ten little snakes, slid over calves and thighs, nestled in the folds of hips and armpits, twined among curls dyed purple (beneath the pubic bone, where the snakelings slithered over moist burrows, snuffled them, but did not slip inside), lashed nipples with their tails, ten nipples in all, curled around them, and bade them farewell. Before gluing his nostrils to the eleventh nipple, the largest and most imposing of any he had ever come across, Joseph Strauss urinated for a long time into a chamber pot as large as a cauldron, behind an arras. Then, biography and all, he sank between Rosa's thighs, trying to abandon there his past.

Belated Prologue

FIRST OF ALL, however, as a sign that kings are anointed by the Lord, not elected by mortals, it came to pass that the young Count of Flanders was laid low by a catarrh. In an armchair by the fireplace that warmed his bones and his eight Christian names—Philippe, Eugène, Ferdinand, Marie, Clément, Baudouin, Leopold, and George—the count rotated a globe between his palms, opened atlases and travel books, sipped an eggnog, dabbed his brow with mentholated tinctures, sighed, and sucked sticks of licorice (*Lakritze,* as he called it, although *réglisse* or *zoethout,* according to his French- and Flemish-speaking subjects respectively) but sweats, fever, sneezes, and the winter beyond the windows made him imagine the throne of the United Principalities of Moldavia and Wallachia as a knobbly stool, cold as ice. Perhaps in other circumstances, had he been in good health, riding or hunting, spurred by springtime to audacious desires and gestures, he might not have hastened to turn down the proposition from the east; he might not have viewed the Romanian crown as something paltry. It was 1866, at the beginning of the second fortnight in the month of February, and the counsels of his worldly-wise father would not have gone amiss. But Leopold had abandoned his realm and family at Christmastide, his body having been lowered into the royal crypt of the Notre Dame Church in Laeken and his soul having ascended to the heavens. The biography he left behind him was blue like a seascape, except that the hue was not marine or cerulean but the deeper blue of royal blood. Born in the Bavarian castle of Ehrenburg, son of the Duke of Saxe-Coburg-Saalfeld, he was a colonel in the Imperial Russian Izmailovsky Regiment at five, a general at twelve, a field marshal at twenty-five (after the campaign of 1815 against Bonaparte), ruler of his native duchy at a tender age, thrice married (to Princess Charlotte Augusta, sole legitimate child of the future King of England, George IV, then to the actress Caroline Bauer, who had hastily been given the title Countess of Montgomery, and finally to Princess Louise-Marie d'Orléans, daughter of King Louis-Philippe I of France), twice a widower, he embarked upon old age amid the tumult of a sordid affair (with Arcadia Claret, paid off with the title Baroness of Eppinghoven), father of six sons and one daughter, stern patriarch, gentle monarch (the first of that newly formed and trilingual state, Belgium), unwavering in the face of military threats and Dutch territorial claims, tenacious in carrying his plans through to the very end (such as the construction of the continent's first railroad, the Brussels-Mechelen line, inaugurated on May 5, 1835), influential adviser to Queen Victoria of England (and author, behind the scenes, of her marital alliance with his nephew, Albert), adept at neutrality in the storm-tossed year of 1848, a man somewhat extravagant in his choice of a future for his only daughter, Marie-Charlotte Amélie, sent across the ocean to be the wife of the Emperor Maximilian of Mexico. In short, a man with ever more strands of gray hair, which later turned altogether white.

It is highly likely that out of this whole series of events, dates, conjunctures, opportunities, calculations, and abilities, the Count of Flanders was thinking of an earlier episode in the life of his father, what one might call a track switch in the life of that prince so preoccupied with railroads. In 1830, at a time when he was not yet called Leopold I of Belgium but merely Georges Chrétien Frédéric of Saxe-Coburg, the duke had spurned another nation's need to bolster itself with powerful characters, titles, and honors, when he declared himself uninterested in the crown of Greece, which had been offered to him on a platter. Now his son, sunk in an armchair, his forehead aflame and his cough worsening as evening fell, administered himself that Balkan precedent as medicine. A physic all the more welcome since he had just discovered that in the northern part of the peninsula, where the map showed the lower course of the Donau (*le Danube*) and some tallish mountains, the Karpaten (*les Carpathes*), philosophy and the belles arts were not much heard of, the balls were modest, and mathematics mostly served for tallying sheep. And so, before dinner, he wrote a letter (in violet ink) rejecting the decision of the two chambers in Bucuresci, the Elected Assembly and the Senate, which, on February 11, at one o'clock, pressed by the lunchtime recess and the national interest, had held a joint meeting and voted unanimously to elevate him to the throne, rechristening him Filip I. In an epoch when not even the swiftest postilion or the most reliable homing pigeon could have made the journey to Brüssel in less than a week, the epistle descended upon the banks of the Dîmbovitza with the speed and force of a bolt of lightning, inducing shudders in three gentlemen and a prime minister, who thus saw their immediate plans thwarted and their longer-term civilizing project hung out to dry.

In the end, those gentlemen, N. Golescu, L. Catargiu, and N. Haralamb—a triumvirate of expedience and members of the Princely Lieutenancy—and I. Ghika, president of the Council, commenced anew their rummaging through the foliage of illustrious genealogical trees, in search of another prince capable of founding a dynasty and taming history. First, however, wearied by events and reversals, fearful lest the disapproval of the future be directed against them, and hopeful that sleep would be a wise counselor, they went to bed, sleeping long but fitfully. They had spent the previous night at the palace persuading Prince Alexandru Ioan Cuza I to sign the act of his abdication, summarily pack his bags, and proceed to the border, escorted by a platoon of alpine troops.

With his unfinished Parisian education in medicine and law, a '48 revolutionary, but first and foremost a freemason, governor of the port of Galatzi, minister of war in the Jassy government, and a proponent of Romanian unification, liberal in his outlook, Cuza had been too much enamored of throne and mistress, forgetful that beyond a certain point some things become scandalous. He had overlooked the farrago in the administration, the plundering of public finances and, more to the point, Russo-Turkish preparations to chant a funeral dirge over the United Romanian Principalities. He had allowed the whitish clouds that continually rose from the land's roads, not only in the wake of carts, carriages, and gigs, but also when little children ran and skipped or hens scrabbled before a rain shower, to settle in a thick layer on the proclamations of the ad hoc Divans. Nine years had passed since the enlightened minds had assembled in frock coats at the urging of the Great Powers, and laying aside intrigue and enmity had examined every facet of the situation, made their calculations, and—weighing every word in order that their will might be clear—placed at the head of their political program two brief statements: *"We desire Unification, but we desire as ardently a foreign prince"* (on the Moldavian side) and *"It is necessary that the ruling prince be chosen from one of the sovereign families of Europe; and this need is imperative and absolute"* (on the Wallachian side). Such were the texts that had been left to gather dust in desk drawers, cupboards, and chests until little by little people began to recollect them, and to fear that this vessel on which they had all embarked might run aground. And the leaders of the lifesaving operation, having risen from their sheets refreshed and clearheaded, quickly changed their strategy. Having burnt their lips and their peace of mind on a soup of Brussels sprouts, the four—General Nicolae Golescu, minister of the interior and of foreign affairs under Bibescu Voda, member of the 1848 revolutionary committee, the provisional government, and the first Princely Lieutenancy; Lascăr Catargiu, with his wolflike senses, honed until then only in appointments as prefect and *en famille;* Colonel Nicolae Haralamb, landowner, son of a court victualler from Craiova; and Ion Ghika, bizarre Turkophile revolutionary of 1848, longtime Bey of Samos—were now so prudent that they would have blown even on a bowl of yogurt before tasting it. Consequently, they did not hasten to pronounce a new name, but extended long, unseen feelers toward the royal courts of the west. They had decided to replace the politics of intuitions, hopes, and *faits accomplis* with one of cautious soundings and discretion. Wandering by circuitous routes over a continent scattered with forests, marshes, snowy mountains, brigands, and military patrols, many of their feelers got bogged down in the wilderness, but others, few in number, found the beaten track to Paris. It was there, in any case, that the conference of the Great Powers was underway, at which the Sublime Porte, intrigued by the rather permissive wind blowing from the principalities, wished to make use of stipulations laid down in the *firman* of November 1861, whereby unification was to be recognized only for the duration of the reign of A. I. Cuza, which was limited to seven years. There were days when one might rightly have said that the souls of the gentlemen from Bucharest quivered like leaves, and the plenipotentiaries of France, l'Angleterre, Turkey, Prussia, Russia, Austria and Sardinia used tones and inflections of voice rarely encountered, resembling the clank of arms. It was also at the close of that February, while ice floes and garbage floated down the Seine, that two of the feelers spread by the Romanian government, the emissaries Ion C. Brătianu and Ion Bălăceanu, gave proof of their skill at snaking through salons, swimming like fishes in the waters of high society, and gaining ingress to all-but-inaccessible bureaus, libraries, and boudoirs. They managed to enchant and flatter. They soothed self-regard, touched sensitive cords, intuited desires and took pains to meet them halfway. And their efforts to elicit sympathy were not in vain, particularly among the ladies, where the decisions that count always come to ripeness. And so it was that the influential Hortense Cornu, the emperor's foster sister, skillfully set in motion a succession of sympathies, first of all drawing into the game the Baroness de Franque. Touched by the fate of that faraway little country, which had barely come into being but was already about to unravel, with its throne vacant and pagans trampling its southern frontier, the baroness passed on the tale with as much passion as if it were a sad novel in which a malnourished and quite possibly consumptive orphan is cast out into the street by villainous bailiffs. Such a narrative could not help but arouse feelings of solidarity, compassion, and affection in her close friend Mathilda Drouyn de Lhuys, wife to none other than the minister of foreign affairs, who happened to be president of the conference now about to come to the boil. It was then a mere formality that, through the long polished mechanisms of conjugal life, the message should be conveyed further. At last, informed and prepared by a creature dear to him, beside whom, as a newborn, he had suckled from the same breast, and persuaded by the chief of his own diplomatic corps, Napoleon III categorically opposed any Ottoman intervention north of the Danube and lent a benevolent ear to the proposals for a Romanian crown. Among the names put forward, four in number, he inclined to the only one allied with the French imperial line as well as the Prussian royal house. Karl Eitel Friedrich Zephyrinus Ludwig of Hohenzollern-Sigmaringen was about to celebrate his twenty-seventh birthday, and as a lieutenant of dragoons in Berlin, he had been waiting for almost a decade to be promoted to captain. Because of the chill he had suffered on a frosty firing range his left jaw had swollen around a decayed molar. The pain was dreadful and, though dizzy, and without consulting his father or Ministerpräsident von Bismarck, he found himself asking the man who was incising his gums with a scalpel whether he would like to follow him to Bukarest, permanently.

Joseph Strauss had never heard of that city and supposed that it must be thousands of miles away, somewhere in the colonies. In any case, the matter seemed to him preposterous and insignificant, especially since in his waiting room two men and a woman were fidgeting on their chairs, and the young officer, given how much pus had accumulated along his jawbone, was probably seeing pink elephants. Later, after lunch, however, the doctor found out by chance that the patient with an abscess as big as a walnut was the middle son of Prince Karl Anton, the military governor of Rhineland, adviser to Kaiser Wilhelm, and recently appointed prime minister. He was amazed. Then, for a good few weeks, he allowed his bachelor's life to flow on in its gentle course between his rented surgery, the room he occupied with Siegfried the tomcat in a sunny boarding house, Der Große Bär, and the Eleven Titties brothel. It was not until April 14, when the daffodils were in bloom and Siegfried had wounded his muzzle and paw in one of the neighborhood cat fights, that he read, to his astonishment, a short item in a gazette about the holding of a plebiscite: "*Today, the lieutenancy and the ministry have proclaimed, by means of bills posted on the streets, the candidacy of Prince Karl of Hohenzollern for the throne of Romania. The event seems to have filled the whole nation with rejoicing.*" That evening, as the jovial Karl of Prussia bantered with the other Karl (now at last a captain) in the foyer of the Berlin Opera House, addressing him as "Turk," the dentist felt no inclination for mugs of beer, for chatter and whist at the bar, or for the eleven titties, two per five lively wenches and the one huge one on the chest of Rosa. Frequently refilling his glass with schnapps, puffing his pipe, and gazing through the open window at the stars and the eaves of the houses across the way, Herr Strauss regretted not having taken the young officer seriously. He fell asleep dreaming of beautiful women and impatient crowds waiting at his door for him to quell their toothaches. A few days later, a courier of the dragoons regiment handed him a yellowish envelope with a crest and the seal of the house of Hohenzollern-Sigmaringen. It was raining buckets, but the envelope was dry when it emerged from beneath the military cape.

2 ❖ The Captain's Shadows

In June, when the solstice draws nigh, dawn is at its earliest. That Wednesday, however, for their eyes no sunrise sprang into view. At dawn, the coach laden with portmanteaus, bags, and trunks set in motion with a judder, one of the horses (a tallish gray mare) whinnied and chomped at the bit, the other (a sorrel with a scar on his throat) puffed out his chest, and from beneath the lid of a wicker basket Siegfried the tomcat mewled heartrendingly. The dentist lost sight of the green shutters of the boarding house, the door, the water barrel in the yard, and the clump of daisies by the gate, but he did see a stripy cat running along the fence tops with fleet and nimble steps, leaping over broken pales, stubbornly keeping pace with the horses. She seemed to him pretty, and large-bellied. At a crossroads, where the coach turned south, the cat must have wearied or floundered in the puddles, because he saw her no more, and soon after, along the streets leading to the Ober-baumbrücke, Siegfried stopped thrashing around and whining piteously and curled up in his basket, with his black ear pricked up and the tip of his tail aloft, while Herr Strauss, whose migraine had not yet relinquished him, gazed through the streaked window at the clouds, the wakening quays, the endless rows of buildings along the banks of the River Spree, the plumes of smoke rising from hundreds of chimneys, and the placid water reflecting a darkling sky, presaging rain. He thought of the hobs sizzling in countless kitchens, he was violently jolted for the length of a bridge, he felt an emptiness in his stomach, perhaps from the rattling of the coach, perhaps from the previous night's beer and champagne, perhaps from the mental image of the sausages, eggs, and bacon being fried in every house, perhaps because of the vista that was now vanishing, as though an unseen hand had wiped away the outlines and colors of a familiar painting.

The storm began at the morning's end, about an hour after the dentist had managed to throw up and rid himself of his grogginess. The lashing volleys of cold raindrops forced them to seek shelter. They stopped at an inn among the hills, where a man and a woman were whitewashing the walls and a lanky girl was halfheartedly scrubbing the floors. By the window, with a mug of warm milk cupped in his palms, Joseph observed how the coachman, soaked to the skin, took care to tether the horses in a spacious shed and to hang oat-filled nosebags from their necks. Inside, the innkeeper wielded his paintbrush with great rapidity, sweating heavily (he kept taking off his tattered hat and wiping his bald pate with a rag), the woman grunted and strained, standing on her tiptoes (hindered by her dumpy body), the girl moved back and forth on her knees, her blouse riding up from the waistband of her skirt (revealing a mole-covered patch of white skin on her back). The whitewash and lye could not drive away the smell of brandy, cider, and smoke in the room. A bitter smell, which rasped against the emptiness in his stomach. An old woman brought lunch: duck soup with peas for him, and the bones and gristle from a chicken leg for Siegfried. The cat did not even touch them.

When the earth had aired a little in the wind and the afternoon sun, the coach set out once more. A light trot that straightaway became a gallop conveyed the doctor into the heart of that rare (blessed? accursed? he had no way of guessing) journey, a convoluted and risky journey, fragmented and odd, which he urged himself to believe would not prove to be an irreparable mistake. The longest journey he had ever taken, and the only important one, so important that he sometimes likened it to a journey to the next world, for after all he was heading to a place of verdure or, at least, a place of golden wheat, endless wheat, as a spice merchant had told him. He was following the trail of the captain of dragoons like a belated shadow, copying his steps and movements at an interval of seven weeks, taking precisely the same route, abiding by his advice, and spending his money. After the epistle in the middle of April, to which he had replied hastily and gratefully with his assent, Herr Strauss had a month later received, from the hand of a lean functionary, another envelope, this time accompanied by a little packet wrapped in waxed paper. Using a paper knife with a silver handle, he had opened both, careful not to break the seals, one familiar, that of the house of Hohenzollern-Sigmaringen, the other unfamiliar, likely the insignia of the new monarch. His former patient, Karl Eitel Friedrich Zephyrinus Ludwig, now elevated to the throne of a land of five million souls, had sent him a pouch of pipe tobacco in which he had hidden so many groschen, guilders, and florins that Joseph had grown faint at the sight, along with a map of the continent on which he had traced out a route in red ink and marked with brown crosses a number of key points. In the letter, he laid out meticulously what Joseph would have to undertake on that exhausting journey, especially since war with Austria was about to break out, and he, a Prussian physician, would have to cross hostile territory, to pass through enemy border posts and checkpoints, to endure suspicion and prying questions. He was asked to conceal his identity, which meant not only procuring false papers, a matter explained in detail, but also one rather laughable duty, namely, getting rid of any petty items that might betray him. Joseph Strauss had obeyed sullenly, even grudgingly, and on one of the days when he was making ready his luggage, he had removed, using a pair of nail scissors, the monograms stitched in his underwear, scraped the letter *S* off his doctor's bag with a razor, concealed a diploma and other documents in the lining of a fur overcoat, and, examining each of his books in turn, torn out the flyleaves that bore his signature.

He parted with the gray mare and the sorrel at Magdeburg railway station. He paid the coachman his fee, allowed a porter to take care of his luggage, and with the wicker basket on his arm went at dusk into a nearby tavern where a greenish lamp swayed above the door. Although he ordered trout in cream, so that they could enjoy dinner together, the tomcat again refused to eat. It was the eleventh time he had done so since their departure. Curled up in a ring, his fur tousled and his forepaws pressed to his eyes, Siegfried seemed very ill. The dentist blinked, lit his pipe, blew smoke rings toward the ceiling, and sipped a blackcurrant liqueur. Then they spent their first night and morning on the train, amid the rumbling of the wheels, the puffing and the whistling of the locomotive, the vernal southern landscapes, the imperturbable amiability of the conductor, and the chattering of a lowly bank agent, who was visiting his sister at a sanatorium in Graubünden. It was not until Zurich, in the attic room of a cheap hotel, that Joseph took his friend in his arms—he stroked him on the crown of his head and under his chin, he clutched him to his breast and spoke to him volubly, he explained to him things that the tomcat surely did not want to hear, for example, why they had not elected to take the railway from the outset but had instead crawled along for a hundred miles in the coach, why they had not headed directly southeast but instead set off southwest, ending up in Switzerland, why a false passport had been necessary, because the drums of two armies were rumbling, the flags of battle were waving, and the troops were on the march, why the landlady of the boarding house in Berlin, his friends, and the girls from the Eleven Titties brothel had had to think he was moving to Stuttgart and not setting out on the trail of an adventurer prince, why a king is a king whatever the state of his teeth, what it means to count out and hold gold coins in your palm, why clocks chime the world over, and, finally, how people grow old. Here, at the words about time and ageing, Siegfried gave a start, pricked up his black ear (the white one remained limp), and lifted the tip of his tail. His master's voice had softened, his caresses had slowed, and the air in the room was growing warmer. Herr Strauss, who in the middle of the previous winter, in January on the eighth day of the month, had turned thirty, was saying all kinds of things, he was not telling a story, he was no longer chirring away meaninglessly, he was merely saying that he wanted to get out of a rut, that there was a whole host of titties in the world, in any case many more than eleven, that everything was numbingly monotonous, that beer and schnapps were good, but wine is not to be sniffed at, that every town is full to bursting with stripy, spotted, black and white, gray, yellow, plump or lean, squint-eyed, and lame cats, cats of every shape and size, that a fire that robs you of a mother and a sister goes on roasting your heart forever, it dries you and smokes you like pastrami, that there comes an hour, all of a sudden, when nothing binds you to anyone anymore, that beyond an empire, three mountain ranges, and boundless plains it is possible to be born again, that to be dentist to a king is not the same as draining the pus from the mouth of a captain of dragoons, that a wife means children, that a new country is a new place, and a new place is a new opportunity, that games of whist can be played anywhere at all, that the present looks like a lump of shit and that the future might, with the mercy of God, look better, that a wife means a mother, that a young tomcat has seed enough to fill the earth with kittens, that beyond an empire, three mountain ranges, and a boundless plain there might not be heaven, but nor can it be hell, that geese saved Rome, that the land where they are headed is called Romania and that there will likely be plenty of goose liver there to fry with slices of apple, black pepper, and onion, that a wife is a sister, that no road is without return, and that a wife means a woman, not just any woman, but one who comes out of an angel's or a devil's egg. And so on and so forth. These were the things that Joseph Strauss said in the garret of a hotel in Zurich, while the room grew blazing hot, and at last he begged the tomcat's forgiveness and fell silent. Siegfried, after sprawling for a while on the chest of that lean, chestnut-haired man, his muzzle resting between the clavicles of that pale, warm-hearted man, looking straight into the eyes of that hazel-eyed, large-eyed man, suddenly leapt toward the window and caught a huge fly on the wing. He swallowed it, then mewled sharply, as though hunger had just pierced his belly.

They feasted forthwith on goose liver prepared in the oven, with slices of roulade covered in sweet paprika, ginger, and acacia flowers, and later they asked for cognac and cold milk: one preferred slow sips, so that he could roll the liquor around the inside of his cheeks and under his tongue; the other favored rapid slurps that sent the cool drink gliding down his throat. Thus they made their peace until peace itself, as a state of affairs, seemed derisory and boring, and then they strolled down tranquil streets, they climbed countless steps and arrived once more in the suffocating garret, convinced that idleness is a supreme virtue, they tasted the sweetness of sleep, one in a bed not quite soft, the other on the carpet in the rays of the sun, and one let out a sigh and the other a mewl when a knock was heard at the door. To Joseph's amazement, into the chamber stepped the same lean functionary who sixteen days earlier, in Berlin, had handed him the envelope with two seals and the little waxed-paper packet. It was only now that they became formally acquainted, as they perspired together, and the eyes of the dentist felt heavy as lead, his attire unseemly. The visitor was called Wolf Dieter Trumpp, and he was the private secretary of Princess Maria, the youngest member of the Hohenzollern family. He seemed not to notice that the doctor was fastening the buttons of his shirt, putting on his waistcoat, and smoothing the creases from his trousers. That gentleman gave a light cough, as though this might have assisted in some way, placed the dentist's new passport on the table, professed his surprise at the hotel's habit of keeping tomcats in the rooms (to guard the guests against mice, he supposed), and explained that the document was in good order, with all the official headings, stamps, and signatures, issued by the governor of the Canton of Saint Gallen himself, Herr Äpli, and not fabricated by some forger. Offering his opinion that a little rain would not go amiss, would reinvigorate the vegetation, the guest also uttered a name, Joseph

Kranich, which the dentist would have to assume for the rest of the journey, this choice of name being the fruit of the governor's inspiration or whimsy, as he had reckoned that an ostrich and a crane, *eine Strauss und eine Kranich*, were somewhat akin. With his hands clasped behind his back, the secretary added that he had made a reservation on the train that left Bavaria on Friday, after nightfall. Finally, Herr Trumpp removed from his pocket a little box covered in maroon velvet, wiped it with his fingertips, and placed it next to the passport. The little lead soldier within, in a victorious attitude of attack, must have once belonged to the young king. It was from his youngest sister, Maria, who had found it hidden under a sheaf of military treatises on his desk in Sigmaringen Castle.

The crossing of the Bodensee was not exactly a joy. The glare out on the lake, the excitement of boarding, the sailors going about their tasks, and the aroma of the tea drunk in the port of Rorschach—all these dissolved under the rocking of that vast expanse of azure also christened the Schwäbisches Meer. The pitching of the boat provoked in the doctor a more wretched nausea than had the beer and champagne, causing him to lean over the side thrice and splatter the water with undigested morsels of his breakfast and a yellowish, bitter juice, such as the foaming streaks of the waves scattered over the lake that also had a third name, Konstanz, perhaps did not deserve. His grogginess had abated by the time they reached Lindau, where he managed, trembling, to gulp down ten drops of quinine mixed with brown sugar, and it definitively dispersed in the mail coach that raced northward, once he had rubbed his temples and the backs of his hands with swabs soaked in vinegar. He spent a night in Memmingen and another in Augsburg, and in Munich he discovered a town as carefree as early summer could make it. He permitted himself a light lunch and hours of delectation, he looked at the ladies out for a stroll, the governesses and the boisterous children, at a group of Dominican nuns, a perspiring bakery woman, and a lass with a bundle of dirty laundry, he indulged his appetite with cherry tarts, he paused in the shade (where his pipe slowly went out) next to a maid perched on a ladder washing the window of a chemist's shop, with her skirt hitched up and a bruise on her left thigh, he leafed through the papers (his pipe now lit), he found time to pause for beer and gaped at some circus folk who were breathing fire, playing tambourines and trumpets, dancing and juggling with colored balls. But in a small square, the thread of pleasure snapped when a top-hatted little dog who was whining in time to music abandoned its performance and, deaf to its trainer, rushed at Siegfried. Two girls screamed, a lady tripped on the train of her dress and almost fell onto the cobbles, a seminary student and a shop boy jumped into a coal cart, an old woman pressed herself against a wall, and the dog, small and dolled up as it was, yapped loudly, bared its gums, growled and snapped at the air. Perched on a fence, the tomcat bristled his tail, spat, and then twisted round and sprayed the dog with piddle.

In the second-class railway carriage where a seat had been reserved for one Joseph Kranich, the doctor spent a very long time deciphering the rhythms and tones of the breathing around him, the cough of the man by the door, the lip-smacking of a country priest, the light snore of a woman in mourning, the fidgeting of a businessman with ginger sideburns, and the unintelligible snatches of speech from a freckled little girl. At Salzburg, as they passed through Austrian customs, he heard his heartbeat, which, oddly, was louder than the ticking of his watch, whose lid was engraved inside with the names of his mother and sister, Gertrude and Irma. The hands showed ten to four in the morning, a cold, damp hour. The wind slipped through the steam of the locomotive, chased away the railway smells, and filled Joseph's nostrils with the scent of lilac. Inside the waiting room, bodies were emerging haltingly from sleep, conversations were being conducted in an undertone, the air was crackling like the guttering candles and dispersing droplets of perspiration, and an officer was bustling ceaselessly, checking the passports one more time, putting stern questions to the travelers, giving orders to the customs guards, soldiers, and his own adjutants. When his turn with the officer came, Herr Kranich was midway through chewing a slice of smoked fish he had found in a handkerchief, left over from the tomcat's last meal. The lieutenant wrinkled his nose, cursorily read the documents, and cast a look of scorn at the brown-haired, unmarried Catholic Switzer with hazel eyes who was heading to Bukarest with the intention of finding gainful employment doctoring Wallachians' teeth. At last, the train glided along the tracks to Vienna—it slipped between troop movements and war maneuvers, it let itself be caressed by torrid heat and fields of ripe wheat, it panted like a supple greyhound loyal to its purpose, it puffed smoke like a young gentleman and became somehow flustered as it neared that city pampered by the fates. Joseph greeted the new sunset dozing in another second-class carriage, with new companions and a new destination, Pest, one of the lungs of the empire, the other being Buda. If someone were rotating a globe in his palms (as a certain count with a catarrh had done that February) or scrutinizing a planisphere, he might have remarked that the dentist had descended a quarter of an inch, at most three-quarters of an inch (some three hundred miles, in fact), as far as one of the soles of the empire's feet, when the railway came to an end and once more the waters of the Danube could be glimpsed. In Baziaş, a gloomy little town dominated by the coal trade, the portmanteaus, bags, and trunk that had set out from Berlin, together with their owner and the tomcat in the basket, boarded a boat for the second time. The passengers' papers were carefully inspected, and so Herr Kranich's profession did not remain unknown to the captain, a fellow with a well-trimmed mustache and a good memory. As the boat passed a long island occupied by a fort, white houses, a Franciscan monastery, and tobacco plantations, an island that was called, in the Turkish tongue, Ada Kaleh, the officer on watch appeared suddenly on the lower deck, called out the name of a migratory bird, and was answered by a pale, thin man holding a tomcat in his lap. He entreated him to come urgently to one of the cabins in first class, where a baroness, a young Russian, was about to give birth. Though he preferred to treat only teeth, the doctor did not hesitate. He hastened to fetch his medical bag and reach the room with sunlit portholes, in which a woman was groaning and trembling, livid, blonde, frightened and astonished, stretched out in bed. Aksinia Larisa Yakovleva was at the end of a honeymoon voyage that had lasted more than a year. The breaking of her water had soaked her dress and the sheets. She was immersed in the throes of childbirth, while her husband, who was older, much older, caressed and kissed her hands, babbling, complaining, weeping in a muffled way, and blaming himself for having miscalculated the length of the pregnancy and for not having delayed the voyage home. Joseph looked at the scene and remained silent for a quarter of a minute. Unimpressed by the baron's laments, Joseph invited him into the corridor and asked him to send for a basin of hot water. Then time progressed like a lazy snail, sometimes curling up in its shell and dozing, sometimes advancing undecidedly, until the baby arrived, just as evening was falling. It was a blond-haired boy who screamed loudly in amazement, and in amazing circumstances: he had Russian parents, he had been delivered by a Swiss (in reality, German) dentist, and found himself on an Austro-Hungarian vessel, with a Czech captain, between the Romanian and the Bulgarian banks of the Danube, both buffeted by winds from Istanbul. At the behest of Osip Afanasievich Yakovlev, the physician tossed back four brimming glasses of vodka and then admitted that he had never supervised a birth before. Plashing the Danube jerkily with its paddles, the steamer had long since passed Turnu-Severin, where he ought to have disembarked, and headed toward Giurgiu, while Joseph slept soundly for two hours, forgetting Siegfried, the young mother, past and future. On dry land at last, he was greeted by a dust storm and dozens of people, some of them barefoot, who jostled him to carry his luggage. It was not until he was in the coupé, jolting along the road to Bucharest, that he found the diamond ring. It was in his matchbox. Next to his pipe. He had seen it on the left hand of the baron, on his middle finger, when they had clinked glasses for the lucky star of the newborn. He laughed.

At first, a diffuse light bathed details and peculiarities; it allowed only outlines and thick brushstrokes to be distinguished, so that their personal histories seemed as alike as two drops of wine. But drops of wine are not like drops of water, and they can have identical forms and colors, but different tastes, for example, a drop of cabernet and a drop of pinot noir. On his way to the Principalities, the captain of dragoons wrote and dispatched letters to the Prussian king, to the tsar, to the French and Austrian emperors, he was accompanied by his trusty chamberlain, von Mayenfisch, by his counselor, von Werner, and by three ordinary servants, he wore spectacles of plain glass, without lenses, so as not to be recognized, he passed everywhere and always as Karl Hettingen, borrowing the name from the family's Swiss castle in Weinburg, once he chanced to find himself in the vicinity of some old friends from the Habsburg army, and was forced to hide behind a spread newspaper, he spent three days in a squalid inn waiting for a boat that had been blocked by military transports, he unexpectedly leapt onto the jetty at Turnu-Severin, in spite of having a ticket to Odessa, and, all in all, countless things in his peregrination happened differently than in the dentist's; the dentist sent no letters, he enjoyed the company of a tomcat, his false name was created by substituting one bird species for another, he did not disguise himself, and he did not glimpse any familiar face. Nevertheless, in the spirit of the times, their journeys were as alike as two drops of different wines. They had followed the same route, they were both Germans, they both had false passports, they both traveled second class, and they both sometimes thought, out of the blue, of the little lead soldier enclosed in a small box covered in maroon velvet.

After they stepped onto Wallachian soil, however, the one on May 8, 1866 (after the Julian calendar), the other seven weeks later, on June 25, nothing was similar. Joseph Strauss did not seek a telegraph office to announce his arrival in his new homeland, he was not treated to a coach drawn by eight horses, he did not cross the Jiu River on a floating pontoon (at dawn, in dreadful weather), he was not greeted in Craiova by a motley crowd and a triumphal arch woven from willow branches, he was not guarded by two files of foot soldiers, and he did not spend the night in a cool manor (making small talk with Zinca, a woman who had lived through much, with her son Nicolae, a Liberal and triumvir, various ministers, and the head of government, the erstwhile Bey of Samos). Joseph entered Bucuresci from the south, through a malodorous slum, in a not at all handsome coupé, in no case coming from the direction of Titu (in a carriage adorned with garlands, drawn by twelve white horses, escorted by a detachment of lancers and followed by a ceremonial procession), he did not wash or attire himself in festive garb in order to receive the keys to the city (outside Băneasa Forest), he did not listen to a speech by the mayor (which went something like this: *Sovereign of Romania! I have given thee the crown of Stephen the Great and of Michael the Brave, thy forbears this day hence! Restore the land to its ancient splendor! Make this beautiful land the progressive sentinel of modern freedoms, the unvanquished boulevard of western civilization!*) and he did not reply in French, stirring first murmurs, then applause, and finally a torrential downpour (after three months of drought). He did not proceed from one end to the other of that long, broad avenue, the capital's only paved street (called Podul Mogoşoaiei), amazed at the potholes, the miasmas, and the buildings, he did not strive to remain upright and composed amid so many jolts, flowers, flags, carpets hung out of windows, cheers (or shouts) from the mob, cannon salvoes and chiming bells, white doves fluttering to the heavens, startled crows flapping, and sheets of paper (calligraphically inscribed with poems) floating like dry leaves in the middle of spring, he did not salute the honorary guard of alpine hunters, infantry, cavalry, and artillery, he did not ask (in front of a one-story house with two soldiers at the door), *"Qu' est-ce qu' il y a dans cette maison?"* and, not having understood the reply, he did not persist, saying, *"Où est le palais?"* He was not greeted on the top of a hill by His Beatitude Metropolitan Nifon (with a gilded cross in his right hand and a silvered Gospel in his left, a synod of priests at his back, garbed in rich vestments); he did not attend mass at the Cathedral of the Metropolia and he did not stride into the main (in fact, rather small) chamber of Parliament to utter the first word of Romanian he had ever spoken in his life (*"Jur!"*—"I swear!") and then follow Manolache Costache Epureanu (in his capacity as president of the Constituent Assembly), who was coughing and clearing his throat, to be proclaimed *domnitor* (in other words, a kind of king) of that land. But, since nothing is perfect in this world, not even differences, their arrivals in Bucharest did have one thing in common. Prince Karl Eitel Friedrich Zephyrinus Ludwig, before being named Carol I, and Herr Joseph Strauss, immediately after arriving in the center of that city, stared wide-eyed in amazement at the numerous swine wallowing in the mud, unfettered and fat, under the very windows of the house that passed as the princely palace. And that was all.

As the twenty-fifth day of June was fading, the clouds of dust were dispersing, and the mounds of garbage were slowly, slowly melting into the darkness, the dentist stopped at an inn by a river, where he was served some very tallowy sausages. That evening he had no strength left to dip his pen into an inkwell. It was not until morning, after dissolving ten drops of quinine in brown sugar and procuring a glass of milk for the tomcat, that he had leisure to write to his benefactor. On one of the days that followed, after he had been received by the sovereign in his office and after the latter, in return for the lead soldier, had entrusted him to a lieutenant of the guard, who was to help him find a place to live, Joseph came across a German street, with all kinds of merchants, functionaries, craftsmen, pharmacists, notaries, bank clerks, jewelers, and watchmakers. It was called Lipscani Street, recalling Leipzig. Soon, the Berliner doctor discovered that he was not the only shadow that had followed the captain of dragoons, as he had, naïvely and without troubling his head, imagined for a while. Around the throne there thronged countless other shadows, among them a physician with the rank of colonel, who had apparently been a foundling; a gentleman named Brătianu, with the initials *I* and *C;* and a professor who spoke very oddly, as if in Latin, though it was Romanian he was trying to drum into the prince. Moreover, Joseph discovered that he was not the city's first dentist. Among romances, poesy, and scientific tomes, he found a slim volume printed in Cyrillic letters, whose reddish cover the bookseller read for him: *I. Seliger, dantist in Bucuresci; Guidance for the Cleanliness of the Mouth and the Preservation of Healthy Teeth.* It had been printed in 1828. He purchased it.

3 ✤ Stained Sheets

WHEN IN YOUR pipe-tobacco pouch there are stashed a copious number of groschen, guilders, and florins, it seems an easy matter to choose a spruce little house and set up a surgery there. Especially if under the floorboards, as a safeguard against hard times, you have a diamond ring hidden away. And Herr Strauss, whom the torrid summer found in precisely such a position, under a munificent star and having managed to pull up one of the floorboards and nail it back again without leaving a trace, had settled in the Saint Nicholas quarter, on the street that teemed with his compatriots, Lipscani as it was named, where he occupied two rooms on the upper floor of a redbrick building. At the same address, number 18, he had also rented the ground-floor shop. It was narrow and long, with a large, shuttered window, a former haberdasher's. He did not dawdle, he began at once to alter it, but not in the two weeks he had thought this would take, rather in five, because the workmen were idlers and drunkards, always ready to demand more money than the initial reckoning. He chased away the first crew one Tuesday, paying them as much as he thought they deserved. From their mouths he heard all kinds of filthy curses (which he intuited, rather than understood), but did not allow himself to be swindled or intimidated. He appeared with a ruler and, taking measurements, making calculations, placed before them a sheet of paper with sums that left them speechless. A few minutes later, Peter Bykow, a baker, knocked at his door, wishing merely to introduce himself, to shake his neighbor's hand and congratulate him on not allowing himself to be tricked. They talked for a little while, as new neighbors and old Germans, clinked glasses of schnapps, laughed, and decided to go rabbit hunting together sometime. Not on the following Saturday, but the one after that, Joseph chased away some new builders who had finished the walls but were lagging over plastering the ceiling and sanding the beams. They departed grumbling. At around lunchtime. Then, after roasted veal and buttered potatoes, after sleep and coffee, while Siegfried dozed fitfully on a sunlit window ledge, Joseph went out into the sweltering air, stopped at a crossroads and drank some kvass, avoided stepping in several piles of horse flop and a reeking dead turkey hen, dodged a cart laden with firewood, went into a tailor's shop and looked at the bolts of cloth (none of them to his liking), bought a poppy-seed cake, and, as he munched, decided to have a haircut. In front of the mirror, while the soft, white linen was draped over his clothes and tucked under his chin, not too tightly, while the shaving brush and razor ambled over his cheeks, while the comb and scissors strolled through his hair, while he was soaped and rinsed with warm water, while he felt palms patting him with an absorbent cloth and fingertips rubbing him with lavender oil, many cloudy things in his life became limpid. This was also due to his chat with Otto Huer, the barber. It was as if he, Otto, had cleansed the inside as well as the outside of his customer's head. From him, Joseph learned the names of two brothers in the Visarion quarter, a painter and a carpenter who worked carefully, quickly, and not too expensively, he learned of an old and skillful stove maker, he found out who it was that had crafted the very chair he sat upon, one just right for a dentist's patients, he learned everything under the sun about grocers, bakers, butchers, druggists, markets, and taverns. They went on talking until almost midnight in a beer hall where they had retired after the cuckoo clock on Herr Huer's wall announced six. Over his first mug, perhaps even over his second, Joseph had listened and grasped how politics was conducted in Bucuresci: theft was the order of the day, until there was nothing left to steal, and no few men, dreaming of the throne, were hoping that Prince Karl would obtain a sizeable foreign loan, fill the treasury, and then go back to his own country. Over the third mug, supping less thirstily, they spoke of how to go about learning Romanian, a sibilant language, sweetened by syrupy vowels, that bore not the slightest resemblance to their own. Mathilde, the sister of Jakob Vogel the optician, had given lessons to many people, not bad lessons, but at that very moment she had the chicken pox and was not receiving visitors. They imagined, as they blew the froth off their beer, a froth as white as milk or Mathilde's skin, how the pustules dotted her face, breasts, and belly button, they pictured how the pox spread over her plump buttocks, like a swarm of red ants or wild strawberries, they sighed, drank and smiled, and then after a while Joseph chased away that image, not from pudor, not because it was not to his liking, but because it was, strictly speaking, medically incorrect. Finally, while they were on the fourth mug, the barber, thinking over other potential teachers—not ones with diplomas, but with compassion and patience—conjured up the image of Martin Stolz: lean, jug-eared, jovial, with a thin mustache and arched eyebrows. He was a notary's assistant, young and eager at all times to lay up a coin in his purse. But because of the shadows dancing on the tin tabletop or the moths dissolving in the flame of the candle, this image failed to imprint itself in their minds. They left Martin to the Lord's mercy, alone in the suffocating, sticky night. They, too, were sweating, yearning for a breath of wind, but still gabbing away. They had lost count of the number of mugs. One said they must have reached their fifth; the other, their seventh. They sighed, quaffed, and smiled. Then the doctor related how one night he had entered a low-ceilinged room, after passing through a courtyard with a chained, lame dog, two goats munching corncobs, and hens sleeping under a fruit tree (plum or quince, who could tell). It had all happened in the dark, the other week, a page now torn from the calendars. It smelled stale and moldy within, he said, and he described how a woman with birdlike eyes had taken off her dress on the threshold, knelt down, opened his trousers and placed his member between her dugs (warming it like a frozen sparrow chick, fondling it). He remembered that, damp and aflame, they had tumbled together on a grubby mattress. In his ears there still lingered the panting, not the sleep, he could not hear that, of course, but he had heard the rustling of dawn. He had not budged, as he saw through half-closed eyes how the woman rummaged through his coat pockets, how she took his last penny (no great matter). Finally, after the sun had risen, he had seen the seamy sheets, stained as if by gobs of spittle. Listening to him with his arms folded over his chest, Otto Huer was of the opinion that in such a city it would not go amiss to have the addresses of bathed, pomaded, and less thievish girls. But neither on that night, over the sixth or eighth mug, nor in the future which then seemed to them so mild, did the dentist ever reveal to Otto the secret of why he had decided to come to Bucharest.

It was on the eleventh day of that August that the young prince who had lured him into a new life next gave a sign. His gums were inflamed, livid, as distressing as bad news. Joseph pushed an armchair to the window, arranged a pillow against the back in the torrid afternoon, and, with a pair of tweezers sterilized in medicinal spirit, extracted a tiny yellow fiber next to one of the prince's canines. It appeared to be from a bean pod. Before he came to perform that elementary but salutary operation, however, and even before he carefully examined the prince's teeth and palatal arch through a magnifying glass, a number of things had taken place, things not worthy of wearying the mind of a sovereign. First, the two brothers from the Visarion quarter, the builder and the carpenter, had turned out to be Russians, not just any kind of Russians, but Filippovian Old Believers, with bushy blond beards, with smocks that reached below their knees and broad belts around their waists, with the foible of not touching strong drink, with blue eyes and a strange religious zeal, who genuflected and kissed the crosses at their throats whenever they ate, quenched their thirst, or heard church bells. They had finished the job rapidly, plastering, polishing and painting, adjusting the window frames and sashes, staining the woodwork with caustic, sanding and waxing the floorboards, glossing the ceiling. It had come out well, hewing to the tastes and blueprints of Herr Strauss, and the price, rightly to say, had been neither so low as to be an act of charity nor so high as to take the coat off a poor man's back. The stove maker too had soon made his appearance, tall and thin, bald, rather like a pottering, peevish heron. He continually chewed leaves, apparently mulberry or wild hemp. He skillfully shackled smoke and straightly joined terra-cotta tile. After the renovation was complete, when nothing in the room recalled the former haberdasher's any longer, Joseph had picked out some Anatolian carpets and affixed to the glossy walls five anatomical charts in gilt frames. He had brought them from Berlin, tightly rolled up inside a flute case. One showed the buccal cavity, including the uvula, tongue, and inner cheeks, another illustrated a mature and healthy set of teeth, and the other three depicted the visible and invisible structures of an incisor, a premolar, and a molar, root and all. He then took care to purchase a pendulum clock, and to give a detailed explanation, at the furniture workshop recommended by Herr Huer, of exactly how he wanted that unusual chair to be: it was to have a single, thick, cylindrical leg in the middle and a screw thread, so that it could be raised and lowered by rotation. It also should have broad, comfortable arms, a neck rest, and a reclining back, like a chaise longue. He had spent an hour and three-quarters sketching the design for the carpenter. Meanwhile, in the forty-seven days elapsed since their arrival in Bucuresci, Siegfried had learned how Wallachian cats held their tails, how numerous the rats were, and how fiercely the stray tomcats fought. He was satisfied, above all because his master had kept his word with regard to the goose liver fried with slices of apple, black pepper, and onion.

By the eleventh of August—the day that his remarkable chair was entrusted to the hands of an upholsterer, who would install its springs and garb it in blue velvet—Joseph had managed to learn a few words of Romanian. And so after he dabbed the prince's gums with tincture of chamomile, he was able to tell him: "*Găsesc fericit tine, Maiestat!*" (I find happy thee, Majestät!)

* * *

Sultan Abdülaziz displayed an unwonted benevolence at the beginning of autumn. Up until then, without being a raging dragon, but rather a padishah astonished and intrigued by events in his northern territories, he had breathed scalding vapors over the Principalities, intensifying the sweltering heat. That breeze had brought with it twenty thousand troops of Turkish infantry, assembled at Rusçuk and ready to cross the Danube on the orders of Omer Pasha. And in the summer (and what a summer!), seeking a smattering of coolness in his new homeland, Carol I had put the army on a war footing, flattered the pride of the national guard on the occasion of the disturbances provoked by the debate of the Jewish question, and abandoned his sumptuous Biedermeier bed, to be found in the little palace on Podul Mogoşoaiei, for one narrower and harder, in the shady residence on Cotroceni Hill. His inspection of the troops and fortifications had left him with a bitter taste, because he had encountered soldiers poorly equipped and devoid of elementary discipline, derisory stocks of cartridges, gunpowder sufficient only to dust the bottom of the sack, horses gaunt and scarce, ramshackle lines of trenches. Now daily wearing the uniform of a general with gold braid and buttons, having renounced that of a captain, the sovereign had also learned alarming details from the report of the minister of war. The rifles purchased in recent years had proved largely defective, the storerooms were bare, new and costly barracks, such as those at Brăila, Galatzi, and Jassy, were in a ruinous condition, the gunpowder factory was rudimentary and unproductive, large sums were being squandered on officers' quarters, and the foundry at Tîrgovişte turned out faulty cannons that were many times more expensive than those imported from the West. There was another figure, too. A gloomy one. Eight thousand. This was how many men that vaudeville army could muster. And the more he came to know places and facts, the more the prince began to discover the muddle and languor in the ministries, the impracticable roads, the impoverished schools and hospitals, the looting and embezzlement in the prefectures, police, and other institutions, how few gas lamps there were in the streets of Bucharest and how many miasmas, the rumors, the string-pulling, and rival camps in politics, the villages like deserted hamlets and the city outskirts like boggy villages, pleasant strolls along the Avenue, the coquettish Cişmigiu Park, where the hand and the skill of a German landscape gardener could be divined, the indolence and dirty tricks of the courts, the tedious evenings at the theatre, a modestly sized and dimly lit auditorium, the thistles in the fields, the dusty market towns, the prisons brimming with the guilty and the not guilty, the resplendent gowns and jewels of the ladies, the cholera that stalked the land like a succubus (and the succubi, in that land, wreaked havoc), the tranquil monasteries of the Wallachian plain, and the splendor of certain landed estates, such as that of the Metropolitan Nifon at Letca. A man by no means tall, with blue eyes, a hooked nose (aquiline, according to some), thick eyebrows, a closely trimmed beard, and beveled cheeks, Karl Ludwig knew very well that neither the state's functionaries nor its soldiers had received their wages since spring. And in the report of the minister of finance, presented to the Assembly, he had circled the following brief passage in red ink:

> . . . *all the official pay offices are empty and the treasury is liable for payment of a fluctuating debt of 55,761,842 piasters; according to a precise calculation, the year 1866 will close with a deficit of 51,956,000 . . .*

In the unrelenting heat, that sentence, the crisis in general, and his Prussian blood prompted him to halve the wages of state employees for a period of six months, decrease pensions, introduce new taxes, and increase the old ones. He was cursed, slandered, reviled, vilified loudly on every street corner, but he swallowed it with stoicism, although he was saddened and the rings around his eyes grew darker. The Great Powers had not acknowledged him as ruler, locusts and secessionist ideas were swarming over Moldavia, Cuza's cronies, stirred up by Florescu and Marghiloman, were hatching dark schemes elbow to elbow with the Austrian and Russian consuls, the French military mission was like a wasps' nest readying its furtive sting, in spite of the good intentions of d'Avril, the consul general, while Moustier, Napoleon III's ambassador to the Sublime Porte, seemed to be acting on instructions from General Ignatieff, the tsar's representative. In one of his frequent letters to Hortense Cornu, his protector in Paris, Carol set down on paper, while sipping wine at around midnight, when he could breathe more easily, the following:

> *. . . this is a land of intrigues, the enemies of order do everything possible to foment unrest. The most dangerous are the Bibescu family, who send secret reports to Drouyn de Lhuys. They behave toward me in the most inappropriate manner and constantly spread slanders. N. Bibescu was saying the other day in company that it is wonderful that Prince Carol has had his photograph taken, because it will be the only thing that will be preserved of him. And the French mission always takes his side . . . The article in Revue des Deux Mondes, where it is said that I am a deserter, was*

published by the Bibescus and the mission. Given that they are
French subjects, the emperor would do a favor to the country
and myself were he to recall them.

And as ever, that lady replied to him loyally and affectionately, honestly and providentially, with the supple ability of
one who works behind the scenes, one knowledgeable about
the details that guide worldly affairs.

In the hundreds and hundreds of lines he read, the former
captain of the dragoons shuddered at many, in the mornings,
on the sofa of his office, as he smoked and drank coffee with
cream, as he opened his correspondence and came up against
the convulsions of the canicular heat. Once he found himself
laughing aloud at this formulation: "*I know that King Leopold*
has cited you as an example of a constitutional prince, but your Ro-
manians are not Belgians." On another occasion, he felt himself
suddenly breaking into a sweat on reading a paragraph that
went, "*the French government looks poorly on the fact that Mr.*
Brătianu has acquired such obvious sway over you and your min-
isters. In 1852, at a time when he was in contact with Mazzini and
Ledru Rollin, Brătianu was involved in a conspiracy against the
life of Napoleon III. I do not condemn him for what he once was,
but now his omnipotence particularly chills your relations with the
people here. I never imagined that you would allow Mr. Brătianu
to rule in your stead, as someone has related to me." In another letter from Madame Cornu, the prince encountered a scintillat-
ing statement, like a flaring match, which caused him to light
yet another cigarette, in excess of his usual morning ration. It
went like this: "*It is said that nothing is being done over there,*
that everything is up in the air, that the recently decreed requisi-
tions have given rise to scandalous thefts on the part of the author-
ities and that these go unpunished. Corruption is the cancer eating

away at the nation. You must extirpate it vigorously." But since the water there flowed under the bridges not of the Seine but the shallow and fetid Dîmbovitza, the prince turned his mind to other matters, leaving the tumor to be excised later. At the end of June, two days after he had stroked with his fingertips and rolled in his palms his beloved lead soldier (received unexpectedly from Maria, via that pale and bewildered dentist), he saw the constitution adopted by parliament, in a stifling atmosphere, as ninety-one fans or newspapers used as fans were raised toward the ceiling of the auditorium, validating with a large majority, in fact unanimously, a law that was in fact the mother of all laws, that consecrated the hereditary in place of the elective monarchy, freedom of conscience, education, opinion, and speech, the right to assembly and association, the inviolability of the person and the home, private correspondence and private property, the indivisible nature of the state, the principles of national sovereignty, representative government and separation of powers, and qualified suffrage. He had hastened to swear a new oath to sanction and promulgate the newborn constitution, and at the close of those hours, to deliver a not particularly ardent speech, a text he had drafted with a cool head, determined not to inflame his audience. Nobody knew (or, if anyone did know, they were few, discreet, and God-fearing) that at the moment when the constitution, silent and smiling, was emerging from the press into the light of day, the ruler's younger brother, Prince Anton von Hohenzollern, sublieutenant in the First Regimental Guard of Prussia, was about to die. He had been wounded in the offensive at Rossberitz, where three bullets had stopped him from leading his platoon's charge, smashed his legs and left him to be taken prisoner shortly thereafter, without, however, snatching from his eyes the gleam (of victory?) or the strength to smile (wanly) when Crown Prince Friedrich in person espied him on a cart for the moribund and shook his hand. He was wrapped in a canvas sheet sticky with blood from the waist down. Two weeks later, when Anton, wearing on his chest the medal bestowed upon him by King Wilhelm, found himself simultaneously at the gates of heaven and beneath a layer of clayey earth, Karl Ludwig revoked the council of ministers, renouncing temporarily, and with bitterness, the services of Brătianu and Rosetti, and, with satisfaction, those of Prime Minister Catargiu, who in a sweltering and blasé Bucuresci was held to be an intriguer, allied with the former prefect of the police and the Bibescu brothers. He then allowed things to flow on in their customary Turkish style, for this was what was needed. In September, with Ghika at the head of the government, he managed to award the Strousberg railroad concession to some deputies who could picture the train snaking and whistling over their landed estates, a business affair that stretched over ninety years and 915 kilometers, departing from Vîrciorova, passing through Turnu Severin, Filiaş, Craiova, and Piteşti, arriving in Bucuresci and continuing through Ploiesci, Buzău, Brăila, Galatzi, and Tecuci, as far as Roman. The project also included the Tecuci-Bîrlad line as a robust, northern appendix, it alone as large as the southern Barkley concession, born exactly one year previously, under Cuza, for the construction of the railroad between Bucuresci and Giurgiu. As for the former Bey of Samos, a man accustomed to the tides and the vices of the Bosporus, to words spoken and unspoken (floating in midair, suspended in the smoke of the hookahs, opaque, sometimes as sharp as a *khanjar*), he hovered like a bird through the torpor of summer, he petitioned the grand vizier and engaged in convoluted diplomatic maneuvers, sufficient to be lucrative but not irksome, and he slipped into the text of the new princely *firman* (which had been kneaded and was now rising like *cozonac*) stipulations such as had never been read or, perhaps, conceived of before. The Sublime Porte recognized the new dynasty and the constitution, granted the young ruler the right to strike coins, and permitted him to increase the strength of his army to a limit of 30,000 men, a threshold neither too high nor too low, but which meant, by virtue of arithmetic, almost four times as many soldiers and officers as existed at the time. And although in that document the United Principalities were termed "*an integral part of the Ottoman Empire,*" vassalage was somehow softened or sweetened by a trifling clarification: "*within the limits fixed by the concessions and the Treaty of Paris.*"

Throughout these events, the prince's wisdom teeth had been niggling, nasty, heartless. And when one of them, out of the blue, took it upon itself to pierce the prince's gums midway through his twenty-eighth year, to sprout on the very eve of his departure for Constantinople, where he was to receive the *firman* of his election and praise the sultan to the skies, to mince his nerves as finely as the meat in a moussaka or the walnuts in baklava, to lead his patience away into barren wastes, and to scatter his sleep over the carpet, when things had come to such a pass, the fact of the matter was that the wisdom tooth was raw in its cruelty. Raw in the full strength and sense of the word. Firstly because the tip of Karl Eitel Friedrich Zephyrinus Ludwig's tongue, feeling the jagged skin, met only a minuscule, rounded bone, as big as a raw grain of rice. Then, because the prince wished not to have raw nerves, but to be calm, lucid, and detached on that journey upon which so many lines and outlines of the future depended. He did not succeed, it goes without saying. He was groggy, exhausted, and overexcited, at the end of a night in which he tossed and turned ceaselessly, opened and closed the window countless times, gargled a liqueur of bitter cherries, drained cups of tea, strove in vain to read or to write to his father, applied cold compresses, then hot compresses, began a chess game against himself, massaged his temples and conceded the first moves, yawned, paced, stretched out in a chair and leapt to his feet once more, took a few spoonfuls of honey, and, at the break of dawn, as a coffee-colored streak fringed the edge of the sky, sent for Herr Strauss, the dentist, his only savior. Urgently summoned by a small cavalry escort on galloping horses, Joseph consented immediately to pack his bags and join the retinue that was to accompany the prince to Istanbul. Later that morning, a long and gleaming file of carriages became rather bogged down on the city's southernmost streets, then wound its way through the stale odors of the outlying slums and the coolness of that ninth day of October, before raising a thick cloud of dust over the plain, a huge cloud that looked like a bushy tail. They startled dogs, starlings, and gophers, and left gap-toothed old biddies open-mouthed, infants champing their lips (in search of the teat), men staring in amazement, and women adjusting their headscarves. It drizzled on the approach to the Danube, to make the point that it was autumn, and the carriages, assembling in four rows, crossed the river by ferry, effortlessly, smoothly, because the whirlpools and currents had abated after such a long drought. Given the cold breeze during the crossing, Carol had chosen not to go on deck. He gazed through the porthole, alert and tense, reclining on cushions covered in cashmere, leaning his chin on his left palm, his right hand clutching his head. He was awestruck by the multitude of flies and midges that swarmed around the horses. In the distance he glimpsed a minaret, gray at first, then milky white as the sun pierced the clouds. He examined the walls of the fortress of Rusçuk, the towers and the lookout posts, the battlements and redoubts, the large pennants, with their undulating golden crescent moons. With his barracks background and incurable passion for order, he could not help admiring the formation in which the troops were drawn up to pay him honor. On the river-bank, near the wharf, he was greeted with a doubtful, barely perceptible smile, a smile that might not have been a smile, but which he, the prince, knew very well could not be any-thing else. Omer Pasha proved gallant, squandering the long and ardent minutes of lunch in praising, through an inter-preter, the precision of Prussian cannons. When at last the de-tachment of soldiers pressed their weapons to their chests and gave the salute, Karl Ludwig felt his throbbing gums erupt, as if the point of one of those slender bayonets had skewered his cheek. Somewhere to the rear, behind the generals, poli-ticians, ministers, advisers, secretaries, and so many others, a muffled thud was heard. A thin, chestnut-haired man with well-ironed clothes had dropped the bag he was holding. It looked like a doctor's bag. Truth to tell, Joseph Strauss had never heard anyone emit such a terrible yowl of pain.

To Varna they were conveyed on a short and motley train, with a red carriage immediately behind the locomotive, like a salon on wheels, with all the trappings of luxury, a blue car-riage in the middle, with broad, restful couchettes, and a green one at the end, used for regular journeys. For six and a half hours—perhaps longer, until one and all they glimpsed the sea, gleaming in the pale dusk, somnolent and boundless— each member of that numerous retinue kept to his allotted place, without transgressing rank or role. As for the dentist, with a notebook in his lap, an inkpot in his left hand, and a pen in his right, he had taken advantage of the company of a garrulous and tic-ridden cook to jot down a large number of recipes, in particular ones for game, fish, and lamb. Even though he understood only a part of the chatter of the lanky man beside him, who had a twitch in his shoulder, blinked incessantly, and accompanied each detail about food preparation with fluttering fingers, Herr Strauss thought gratefully of young, jug-eared Martin Stolz, with his thin mustache and skillful Romanian lessons. He did not, however, know the words for something essential in the language, the names of the condiments, and so he had patiently tried to elicit them, in that train advancing over hills and through forests, tilled fields, pumpkin patches, hay meadows, and vineyards, now crawling through oriental-looking towns, now hurtling past isolated houses, villages, and flocks. Onerously, he managed, amid a welter of words and a flurry of gestures, to discover the words for pepper (*piper*), mint (*mentă*), paprika (*boia*), garlic (*usturoi*), rosemary (*rozmarin*), poppy seed (*mac*), and tarragon (*tarhon*). They had got as far as lovage (*leuştan*), boredom, and the impossibility of matching up in German all the aromatic herbs and seeds of Romania, when Joseph was summoned to the first carriage, the red one, where Prince Carol, anticipating the moment when he would acquire, peruse, and decipher that enchanted document (which must have looked like any other document but which would, at last, bestow upon him genuinely sovereign powers), was pacing like a caged wolf, oblivious not only to the landscape and people, but also to his own attire. The top three buttons of the prince's waistcoat were undone, his belt was loose, the buckle drooping by his hip, and he was wearing lilac slippers with curved, pointed toes and silk tassels, while his immaculate black boots awaited him under a coffee table. They remained alone together for a while. The prince was walking from one end of the room to the other, his head slightly bowed, his paces measured and equal in cadence, nineteen paces forward and nineteen paces back. He always turned on the sole of his right foot. Nineteen paces to the southeast and nineteen paces to the northwest. All of a sudden he stretched out on the narrow couch, for such was now his whim, and lay with his eyes fixed on the ceiling. And upon the arching ceiling was emblazoned a silver crescent moon, framed by meticulously engraved and painted chains, lines, and spirals, as if the red car gliding down the iron rails of the Ottoman Empire might at any moment have transformed itself by the mercy of Allah into a small, mobile mosque. The dentist rummaged among his flacons, powders, and instruments, and selected a curved pair of tweezers, lint, medicinal spirit, and extract of celandine. In a few minutes, he managed to lull the prince's wisdom tooth to sleep, or at least he persuaded it to doze. He was getting ready to withdraw, but Karl Ludwig, who according to some had an aquiline profile (and perhaps he did, but not then, lying on the couch groggy and perspiring, with deep bags under his eyes), begged him not to leave. They examined together one of the lilac slippers, they discussed at length and in German its shapes and details, they presumed many things and strove to imagine even more, until the slipper, with its curved, pointed toe and silk tassel ceased to be a mere slipper and became an embodiment of the world that Karl Eitel Friedrich Zephyrinus Ludwig had entered five months previously, a world in which he often wondered what he was looking for, in which he was sometimes astonished to find himself. Herr Strauss, meditating on the fate of the prince and that land of plentiful goose liver, of more barrels of wine than beer, of charlatans and cereals, of tumult and tobacco, permitted himself to offer the not at all reassuring advice that he should keep his poise, his determination, and his throne. Carol cleared his throat, shook Joseph's hand with unwonted firmness, and asked (he did not command) that the dentist find an appropriate (and blessed) remedy for his tooth prior to his appearance before the sultan. After they parted, Joseph found himself in a quandary; he had left on the other side of the upholstered door a man agitated, exhausted, and fearful. In the rear car, with its second-class insignia and rhythms, the cook was snoring gently, his brow resting on the windowpane and his shoulder still twitching. They had not yet come to any agreement about whether *leuștan* was lovage, but the hours and the days had not yet run out.

In the time it took the train to reach the coast, the sea had, in succession, been tinted by the nacreous hues of sunset, the ashen tones of the gloaming, the dark visage of night, the reverie of sunrise, and the azure splendor of a new morn. Now at last it revealed its many faces, as various as the seasons, to a ruler who was and was not a ruler and to generals, politicians, ministers, advisers, secretaries, and plenty of others who also were and were not what they believed themselves to be. That morning, many were viewing the sea for the first time, for which reason some of the officers and servants made the sign of the cross and each placed a stone in his mouth (a small one, of course, as big as a cherry pip or a raisin). A few knew the sea well, from voyages and paintings, and there was one among them who felt it was like a woman with whom he had shared his bed sheets for many years, a boyar, the one who, in the chill of autumn and old age, passed for prime minister, having previously devoted himself to engineering, secret societies, revolution, and literature, to high office and wine, a man famous above all for being the erstwhile Bey of Samos. By noon of the following day, the tenth of the month, they contemplated, from dry land, the waves as they shimmered and dissolved into spray. Then, in the early afternoon, they gazed upon the billows as they rose and swelled on the open sea, from the deck and through the portholes of the schooner *Yssedin*. Those endless undulations, in which the rays of the sun dissolved and transformed into ripples of light, bewitched not only souls but also stomachs, so that on the two-masted vessel, one among the countless velieros of the padishah, on board which they had been greeted by an adjutant general, no few were those who sought pots, troughs, and basins, retching as they furtively rid themselves of what remnants of lunch they still preserved inside them. The dentist enjoyed the cruise, but seeing the others he could not help remembering his crossing of that lake with three names (Bodensee, Schwäbisches Meer, and Konstanz) and his own sufferings. In contrast to the Swiss episode, however, when he had been able to opt for water and fresh air instead of buckets and nooks, here no one dared to lean over the rail, so as not to sully the blue expanses or annoy the matelots of the imperial Ottoman fleet. And the Bosporus was revealed to them after two more sunrises, to some as a wonder, to others as a strait overrun with ships and barges, girdled by land of every variety: summer residences seen through the filmy sheen of October, arid beaches and shorelines, yellowed orchards and vineyards, fishing villages. The great city was close by, its exhalation was like a breeze, and Joseph Strauss, who was changing the cold compresses on the cook's forehead, knew what he had to do. He opened his ruddy calfskin bag, from which, not long ago, in June, he had scraped the letter S, grasped his scalpel, and made an incision in one corner of the lining. Underneath, in the very spot where he was poking his index finger, he found what he was sure he would find. Then he went on tending to the livid, lanky Calistrache, who had managed to explain to him what *leuştan* (lovage) was, but had faltered at *chimen* (caraway), *leurdă* (ramson), and *rău de mare* (seasickness). It was not until he was inside a servant's chamber in the Küçüksu Palace that Joseph removed from the lining of his bag a small brown envelope and slipped it into his breast pocket. He read a few pages from Leibnitz about optimism, he thought of his mother and sister, Gertrude and Irma (who had been so enamored of that tea that they had sunk into beatitude and indolence, not noticing either the fire or the smoke), he lit two incense sticks on the nightstand, in memory of them, and when the news came that the Glorified Sultan was ready to receive the prince, he sprinkled into some boiling water a quarter of a teaspoon of the fine powder concealed in the brown envelope. It was *Amanita muscaria*, which he had prepared himself, gathering the white-flecked red mushrooms, peeling their cuticle, drying them in the darkness of the attic of his Berlin lodgings, chopping them finely, and crushing them with pestle and mortar. Karl Ludwig, the prince, blew on the piping hot liquid, sipped it, and did not set off on the visit that was giving him frissons until he had drained the cup. He made another, short voyage on the Yssedin, from the coast of Asia to the coast of Europe, and after the anchor had been cast he was transferred to a velvet-upholstered *kayik* with twelve rowers. He was wearing a parade uniform, that of a general of the United Principalities. All of a sudden he felt like giving a whoop, and could not refrain. And give a whoop he did (to the astonishment of politicians, ministers, officers, advisers), as he finally, belatedly saw the tranquility of the sea and sky spread before him, and glimpsed the white palace stretching for two thousand feet along the strait, so familiar in its outlines and ornaments (for it had borrowed a number of features from Versailles and had closely copied the architecture of the Neues Palais Sanssouci). His lungs filled not with the salt scent of the breeze but with the air of childhood, and he was oblivious to the final advice of the adjutants and to the recapitulation of the ceremonials laid down for the audience with the padishah. He had forgotten his aching gums, absorbed as he was in the crinkled seaweed and the seagulls. On one of the marble-paved esplanades of the Dolmabahçe Sarayı, that Prussian prince, a Wallachian by adoption, who had arrived from the northern bank of the Danube but also, to be more accurate, from its very source, was saluted by a platoon of the guard. It seemed to him that not one of the soldiers with red fezzes resembled his little lead soldier. He was then conducted down a bright corridor, at the end of which Sultan Abdülaziz was waiting for him, with a calm and calming face, as his siesta and the events of the afternoon had probably been to his liking. He stood in the doorway, extending his hand to the prince. And from that moment, when the infusion of *Amanita muscaria*, or *Fliegenpilz*, began to take full effect, nothing turned out as it ought to have, in accordance with rules and rituals. Carol did not kneel and he did not kiss the hand proffered with such magnanimity; he merely inclined his head and shook the hand in a comradely fashion (as if he were in the barracks of the dragoon regiment), he did not take his place on the chair specially prepared for him, but pushed it aside and sat next to the sultan (on the soft, restful divan), he proved to be voluble, highly voluble, answering questions at length and in a muddled way, and pressing the padishah for his opinions (not those of the most serene ruler so much as those of a man blessed with a harem), he was not at all distracted when he was handed the *firman* of his appointment (that longed-for and enchanted document), but placed the *hatti-şerif* with the imperial seal on a table and went on describing an opera performance (*Die Zauberflöte*, in Bremen), he did not wait for Abdülaziz to enter the antechamber to be introduced to the distinguished members of the delegation from Bükreş, but hastened to call his ministers into the salon, asking the minister of foreign affairs, not the prime minister, to pick up the *firman* and place it about his person, he declared himself fascinated with the Bosporus and Istanbul, but above all with the seagulls, the crinkled seaweed, and the brightly glinting roofs. Although at the time his behavior provoked bewilderment and fear among his subjects, soon and forever afterward it was interpreted as dignified, audacious, canny, and incomparable, a sign of noble blood and devotion to homeland. And that afternoon, Karl Ludwig slept soundly and dreamed that he was riding a gray pony, then that he was shooting his pellet gun at wooden targets in the shape of hares, boars, and foxes. He awoke toward evening in a spacious room of the Küçüksu Palace. On the *secrétaire* by the window the *firman* of sovereignty was awaiting him, bound in leather, stitched with gold thread, written on waxed pages in the impeccable calligraphy of the Ottoman scribes, with the seals of the Sublime Porte and the curlicues of the Sultan's signature. He had a severe headache, and his wisdom tooth had also recovered its vigor. For a week, in spite of his demands for another cup of that sweetish infusion or at least its recipe, he had to content himself with extract of celandine. He conversed with the dragomans and ambassadors who arrived for audiences. He strolled at leisure around Constantinople. He tried a number of times to count the mosques, but would always get mixed up on account of the minarets, with one or more for every place of worship. He visited the all-powerful Abdülaziz twice more, full of gifts and reservations, without confessing his desire to see the bird pavilion or the huge reception hall of the Dolmabahçe Sarayı, with its fifty-six stone columns and its gigantic chandelier, weighing four and a half tons. Following the logic of gestures of goodwill, Carol received a Damascus sword and five Arabian stallions, he was decorated with the Order of Osmania and invited to attend a military parade. During a cold rain, Prince Yusuf, eleven years old, with a reedy voice and two superior officers holding the reins of his horse, presented to him the battalion. The rain began to fall more heavily, allowing the treasurers to dip their quills in their inkpots, put all the expenses down on paper, and tot them up. All in all, and also taking into account bribes, the trip to Istanbul had cost 20,000 ducats, which is to say 240,000 francs. But the price of obtaining the *firman* was much greater, because from that year forward, the one thousand eight hundred and sixty-sixth year since the nativity of Christ, the tribute payable by the Principalities was to increase substantially.

In the green railroad carriage, on the return journey, Herr Strauss inquired, offhandedly, as if merely to pass the time, whether the cook had heard of a poisonous white-flecked red mushroom, *Fliegenpilz* in German. In Romanian, he discovered, it was called *pălăria șarpelui* (snake's hat). Or *burete șerpesc* (snake mushroom).

Thanks to you, good Otto, who suffered to receive the keys to my house, who fed me and gave me water, who cleansed me of much red blood, who guarded me from the hostile tomcats, praise be to you, O barber, who have comported yourself like an angel and, in your great mercy, have always unbolted this door, and a while after the departure of my beloved master, when for the fifth time the day broke after the night, did once again open the locks and not only bring meat, gristle, and milk, but also released from your arms as if from under your unseen wings a peerless girl-cat, trembling as though at the beginning of the world and sighing as though at the end of the world, you, O barber, you alone gave me the gift of love, all unawares, when I was hungry, you caused me to shiver and quake, your miracle was real, a maidenly and tender cat, Ritza, as you yourself and other humans call her, Manastamirflorinda by her true name, may you be rewarded, Otto Huer, for your deed, for in fear and wonderment did I approach her at first, her tail stood on end and her back bristled like a hedgehog's, ruddy spots smoldered in her fur, like embers, her scent was more beautiful than fresh fish or pigeons, she gave a start when my nostrils snuffled her, when they imbibed her perfume, I know not why, perhaps out of fear, but I sought to soothe her with my tongue, you understand, O barber, for you have much experience, but that inspection was not to her liking, and I stretched out on the floor, my eyes closed and my ears flattened, at a distance, under the five-drawer dresser, because my wound wracked me once more, the pain shot even from my heart, and know you, dear one, that sometimes time flows briskly and the hours tick merrily, I sensed her breathing between the strokes of the pendulum clock, warm and gentle, like an April breeze, and she, Manastamirflorinda, licked my white ear at length, the ear torn by a cruel and furious tomcat, the ear that you, O benefactor, cleansed with one of my beloved master's potions and stitched with his healing thread, she nestled beside me, the ruddy spots in her fur were glowing, we were silent, then we sang softly, a duet, be not angry, O barber, but never could you have suspected, you would have thought that we cats were purring, but we were singing and we opened our eyes, one after the other, eye to eye, her green eyes were

boundless, like vernal fields full of gophers, peace be unto you,
once more, good Otto, O magician, for you are a magician
and all that came to pass was a spell, for seven days through
which processed six nights we dwelled in tenderness, we rolled
together on the carpets and we dissolved into one, we scaled
tables, cupboards, and dressers, seeking tenderness and repose,
once we almost fell, from the stove, but we caught ourselves,
our forepaws entwined, our tails likewise, mine white with
a black tuft, hers black with a ruddy spot, we dallied in the
bed of our beloved master, at leisure, having slipped under the
soft coverlet, so that it would be dark and that the world be
contracted thus, I would not have wished, O barber, you to be
witness, because you would have shuddered to hear us, they
were the rustlings of love, not meows; Manastamirflorinda
and I were center and circumference, our bodies on the upper
floor and our souls in the firmament, we were in the belly of a
fluffy cloud, from above which you, dear, merciful Otto Huer,
did descend, turn the keys, and enter, you did stroke us and
sigh, you did fill and drain three glasses of my beloved master's
schnapps, you did wrap the maiden in a tartan rug, in the
evening, when she was a maiden no more, you did take her in
your arms as if between your unseen wings and vanish, praise
be to thee, O angel, may thou be rewarded!

Thusly and thus much wrote Siegfried on yellow velvet
before falling into a deep sleep. He had inscribed his psalm on
the back of one of the new chairs, and his soul and ten claws
had not been idle.

Herr Strauss arrived in the morning, weary, his clothes
rumpled, dreaming of a hot, interminable bath and a milky
coffee. He called the tomcat from the doorway, still holding his luggage, ready to kiss him and to regale him with the

smoked swordfish he had brought from Istanbul. But Siegfried was nowhere to be seen. Herr Strauss had time to take off his overcoat, light the fire, and put the kettle on the stove. He opened the windows wide, enough to let the cool of the twenty-third day of October waft into the room. Long did he gaze outside, and he called out once more, but the street was bustling with people, horses, and donkeys, not at all an hour for stray cats. He was about to tear the leaves from a calendar, quite a number, for after all he had been gone two weeks, when his eyes alighted on the back of one of the chairs, which was covered in hundreds, perhaps thousands, of rips, rents, slashes, and holes, as if the velvet had been riddled by moths or pecked by sharp-beaked birds. He did not even shrug. He merely stood there, mute, heedless of the boiling kettle. Later, he espied a hummock in the middle of the bed. He found the tomcat under the coverlet, asleep on the white sheets, sad and ill, curled up over a hardened bloodstain. Examining the wound on his ear, touching the stitches, and running his fingers through the cat's fur, Joseph was convinced that Siegfried had lost, if not the war, then at least a number of street battles, and that he had suffered from loneliness and longing. It did not enter his mind that the dried black blood might be that of a young she-cat, who had recently come into heat for the first time.

In the kitchen, on the top shelf of the sideboard, there were other scratches. Those notches in the wood, which were to fill with dust but never fade, read in translation something like this:

> What wonder, and what fortune, and how all things
>   followed upon one another, and now more than ever
>   would it seem rich to die

The rustling has not faded, I see it, it is the mist that floats through the room
The moonlight lolls on the floorboards, I hearken, it quivers like Manastamirflorinda
The droplets of sadness, I smell them, they wax large and ruddy, they are the very flecks in her fur.

The German Christmas came, dismal and damp, with days not cold enough for the sleet to turn to snow. And on one such day, luminous only in things holy, boots sank into muddy puddles and hurried carriages splashed capes with splatters of brown. Time was measured in different ways in Bucuresci, and this year the Catholic Christmas Eve, when wet, skinny dogs had been lured to the Lipscani quarter by the scent of roast goose, baked carp, *cozonac,* and gingerbread, coincided, in the Julian calendar, with the feast of Saint Spyridon, which maddened the cats, for it fell in the fifth week of the Orthodox fast, bringing a dispensation to eat fish. And so it came about, when December 24 and December 12 were one and the same day, that the different calendars, one Western and the other Eastern, one Papist and Protestant, the other Orthodox, were at peace as never before. The two separate holy days did not merge into one common feast, but at least the shutters of all the shops remained closed. As a good Catholic, Joseph Strauss, the dentist, whose surgery was, it goes without saying, closed, said his prayers, and then leaned on the sill of an upper-floor window to gaze at the clouds, crows, gray roofs, and the smoke that rose from the chimneys and dissolved to the north. He nibbled on a sweet-cheese strudel, feeling languid from the heat of the stoves and the tidiness that the woman who came to do the cleaning, infirm as she was, had managed to instill in his bachelor rooms. In the six months he had been living there, he had learned sounds and distances, details and echoes, so that the first bell he recognized, in the cold drizzle of that morning (not quite sleet, not quite hail), was that of the church at the end of Podul Mogoşoaiei, joyfully chiming to announce the feast of its patron. And because all things can be divided into old and new, not only calendars, shoes, reigns, maids, potatoes, and mistresses, immediately after the soft, delicate chimes from the old Church of Saint Spyridon there resounded the long, booming clangs of the new Church of Saint Spyridon, at the foot of Metropolia Hill, where the celebration was officiated with greater pomp. Then, one after the other, each of the bells of the city began to chime, until they were all ringing in unison, summoning folk to the liturgy and love of God, a reminder that in that land the Orthodox faith was strong and the founders of churches who dreamed of forgiveness for their sins were countless. Unawares, Herr Strauss murmured something hard to make out, a passage from the *Dominus dixit ad me,* and out of the blue, or out of the damp gray sky, he glimpsed another Joseph, thinner, shorter, with a shrill voice and flushed face, in the balcony of the Sankt-Hedwigs-Kathedrale on Bebelplatz, in the third row of the choir. For a few moments the doctor once more inhabited the child's body. And he was happy. Then, still with the strudel in his hand, his upper lip dusted with icing sugar, he listened to the majestic voices of the humming and vibrating brass. His thoughts were borne off on the wind, southward, past the churches of Saint Anthony the Great, Saint Demetrios, and Saint John the New, they skirted Stavropoleos Monastery, by the banks of the dirty, sluggish river they met the spires of the Dormition of the Mother of God, of the Holy Apostles and Princess Bălaşa, they found, on the right hand and the left hand of the Metropolia, Antim Monastery,

Mihai Vodă Monastery, and the Nuns' Hermitage (where he had bought a carpet in September), and the churches of Saint Nicholas Vlădica, Slobozia, and Saint Catherine. Climbing to the east, as if his ears were following a course opposite that of the sun, he wandered in his mind to Saint Venera, Saint Mina, Old Saint George, Răsvani, and New Saint George. Soon he veered northward and smiled to realize that in the part of the city that corresponded to the cardinal point cursed with cold and shadow, the names of laymen and things were favored for churches above those of the saints: Colţei ("pitchfork"), Scaune ("thrones"), Kalinderu ("calendar"), Batiştei ("court-yard"), Sărindar, Enei, Kretzulescu, Doamnei, and, only after that, Saint Nicholas Şelari ("saddlers"), Saint Sava, and Saint Nicholas dintr-o Zi. From the west, where the circle imagined by Joseph Strauss came to an end, there came only two series of chimes, one hollow, the other honeyed, from Saint John the Great and from Zlătari ("goldsmiths"). Then the bells fell silent, each according to its tongue, but only after the Un-clean One had been driven from every place. In the damp air the silence was consummate, though raindrops were pattering upon the sill and Siegfried was growling in his sleep, dream-ing of hounds, hostile tomcats, and rats. Joseph had finished munching the last morsel of strudel, and now he sank into an armchair and began to read Apuleius' *Metamorphoses, or the Golden Ass,* sipping a glass of cider. Gradually absorbed by the misadventures of the young Lucius, he forgot the packed churches redolent of incense, whose number was known only to a few, perhaps only to certain priests and tax collectors. As he smoked a quincewood pipe, he was not thinking about how everywhere in that sprawling city, as far as the barriers toward the open plain, sermons were praising Saint Spyridon, Bishop of Trimythous, who had changed a snake into gold pieces, who had called forth rain in the midst of drought, and who, raising from the dead two horses with severed heads, found that he had attached the white head to the dun horse and the dun head to the white horse.

Later that gloomy afternoon, the dentist tried to sleep, but tossed restlessly under the sheets, his eyes closed. Faces, phantasms, gestures, events, appearances, and deeds came all in a welter, without connection or logic, each enveloping him in turn, tender or paroxysmal, then vanishing as mysteriously as they had arisen. He had barely twisted onto his side and settled the pillow under his right cheek when he remembered the fantasy he had had in April in Berlin, in which beautiful women and impatient crowds waited at his door for him to quell their aching teeth. He had a few patients, some regular, some occasional, but he had understood from the outset that one of the local vices was that people did not care if they were gap-toothed. They did not brush their teeth, they ate as best they could, and they hastened to have bad teeth pulled. They pulled their teeth themselves, having first steeped them in plum brandy, *mastika*, rye brandy, and raki, or they went to barbers who wielded chisels and large pincers, whom they called toothsters. Such customs left Joseph with a bitterness in his mouth, one he could taste even then, in bed. He turned over onto his tummy and lost himself in a late autumnal landscape. Once again he saw a gray rabbit bound from behind the bushes and run zigzagging over a ploughed field, cleaving the fine mist, then suddenly encountering a bullet from the gun of Peter Bykow the baker and spinning over the clods of black earth. A dog fetched it, and Peter wrapped it in burdock leaves and crammed it into his pouch, alongside another four. On the Ciumernicu estate where they had hunted in the whitish light of dawn, queer shapes and outlines loomed, colored like the cold. The two Germans, one with a scarf and fur-lined cap, the other with a rifle slung over his shoulder, had come to a stop on the Wallachian plain, at the edge of a village of Bulgarians, and were gazing at a stocky, bald man wearing priestly garb, who was piling thick layers of straw onto some vine stocks. He was working slowly, with a pitchfork. He greeted them in Slavonic and Latin, then Romanian, mentioned his name in passing, and, in that mixture of languages, confessed that he was fearful of the frost, the angels' anger, and the darkness. He left his horse hobbled on the stubble field and led them to some low-roofed houses, beyond which lay the manor of the boyar Condurat. On the way, Necula Penov, the priest, talked continuously (pausing only to cough): about how the pumpkins grow, how for eleven years he had held services in a sheepfold, how they planted peppers and cauliflowers, how he administered the sacraments, how he scared away the crows, how he arranged christenings, and how, day after day, he confidently awaited a letter from the magnanimous and kind Pius IX, in reply to the one hundred and seventy-six epistles he had sent to the Vatican. At a crossroads shaded by tall poplars, the two hunters, a dentist and a baker, subjects of that same Pope, discovered to their astonishment that the ramshackle structure before them, with an iron cross on the peak of its roof, bore a blessed name: the Virgin Mary Queen of the Holy Rosary. It was a church of planks and earth, clad with reeds, Catholic in accordance with the desire of those peasants who had arrived from south of the Danube in 1828, during times of war. In his warm room, Herr Strauss also glimpsed the churchyard, swarming with sparrows as if there were grains of millet strewn throughout the grass. In the end, he did not find the path that led to sleep, and so, enervated, he emerged from between the sheets as the light outside was beginning to fade. He heated some water, readied his razor, shaving brush, soap, two towels, and clean linen. He washed thoroughly and shaved with care, meeting his hazel eyes in the mirror, eyes free of sadness and worry. When he went out the front door, he was wearing a gray coat, hat, and galoshes, and the hour hand of the pendulum clock rested halfway between five and six. Beneath the drizzle, Lipscani Street resembled a river, along whose course calmly flowed not water (puddles and pools), but people. Joseph walked side by side with the others, warmed by the throng. He heard snatches of conversation, replies, stray whispers, many in German, but plenty in Italian, Hungarian, and Polish, and even the laughter of some young ladies, whom he avoided. At one point, the river split into two branches, one swerving strangely uphill, as no river can do, toward the Lutheran church, the other flowing onward, down a gentle slope. And outside the walls of the Catholic Church there had gathered so many souls that for a few moments he could hardly believe his eyes. He found a place to one side of the door, out of the way of those who were still arriving. He climbed onto a heap of coal and looked out, scanning the fresh darkness. Amid the wet capes, umbrellas, and cloaks, he descried the profile of Mathilde Vogel, now cured of the chicken pox. At that distance he could not make out much, but it appeared to him that her cheeks were rosy and her chestnut curls were touching her earlobe. He wondered whether it was worth pushing his way through the crowd, whether the cold raindrops bathed her or bothered her, whether her boots were dry, whether her calves were quivering and puckering. He was thinking of many things and standing motionless when the first bell chimed loudly, the largest bell, donated to that church, Sancta Maria Gratiarum (Holy

Mary Mother of Grace), by none other than Franz Josef, the emperor in Vienna. Soon, in the white tower, the smaller bells also began to ring, bells fashioned at the behest of the august sovereign Archduke Franz Karl and Princess Sophie, bidding peace between couples and contraries, and after them, the smallest bell, a gift from Maximilian, brother of the Austrian emperor and an emperor in his own right, at the other end of the world, in Mexico. The chimes heralding Christmas Eve pierced the clouds above Bucharest and, the dentist thought, dissolved in the glassy firmament, rising to the stars. Also there rose the music from the beginning of the Liturgy of Angels, *Filius meus es tu, ego hodie genui te,* and the chords of the organ struck the windows of the cathedral, then trickled through the wide-open doors, touched the bowed heads of the crowd, kindling voices and hearts, and in a corner of the churchyard, by the gate, tears gleamed on the face of Herr Strauss. Together with the others he intoned *Laetentur Caeli* and *Tecum principium,* plunging with his spirited voice into the spell of psalms 95 and 109, and at the end of the service when the calm river began to flow backward, from the Catholic Church to the congregation's houses, he strove to meet up with Mathilde, but glimpsed neither her nor her brother, Jakob Vogel the optician. So he stopped off at his own house instead, helped Siegfried to climb into his wicker basket, and carrying him on his right arm, he headed toward the home of his friend Otto Huer. They all sang in chorus, and even Siegfried purred along, by the stove. They drank raki and wine, they feasted on countless dishes, above all that steaming wonder, *die Weihnachtsgans,* roast goose. They remembered the old, the sick, and the poor, and even the ravenous stray dogs, for whom they filled two pots with bones. And they prayed for them all.

A carriage had waited in front of the redbrick building, Number 18 Lipscani, for an hour and a half. A lieutenant of the guard, with sideburns, had orders to hand the dentist a note. It was from the prince, inviting him to the palace for tea by the Christmas tree in the library.

In the Yuletide atmosphere, spending Christmas for the first time far from his family, Prince Carol had announced during the course of the evening that he was not feeling well, and had withdrawn to his office, refusing all company. For hours on end, without rising from his desk, he set down on paper, in five versions, many of the things that had burdened him in recent months. With varying degrees of intimacy, occasionally sipping a bitter cherry liqueur, he wrote in turn to his father, mother, sister, and brothers, adjusting tone and nuances to the face and personality of each addressee in mind. Events were compressed or detailed; descriptions that were cold in one letter grew impassioned in another. He placed the emphasis now on politics and affairs of state, now on feelings and sorrows. Sometimes he revealed himself to be strong, poised, and optimistic, sometimes he bemoaned his fate and gave free rein to his doubts. And in all the different versions of his brief history as monarch, one each for Karl Anton, Josephina, Leopold, Friedrich, and Marie, he referred to the large Oppenheim loan, the finishing touches to which had been made in Paris after his confirmation by the Sublime Porte, a lifesaving transaction that quelled the protests of officers and functionaries, even if it did involve the repayment of 32 million francs over twenty-three years, on a principal of just 18.5 million. Then he related how the elections to the two chambers of parliament in November had been not only an occasion for brawls, abuses, and manipulations but also depressing in their outcome, which had left the government without serious support. Likewise, in disappointed terms he described the first palace ball, held at his own personal expense, an act of normality and decency in his opinion, but also a target for vile attacks, on the grounds that he had squandered the country's money in a period of grinding poverty. Finally, long after nightfall, when the loneliness had become oppressive, the prince felt a need to chat and to forget. Smoking a cigarette, he thought of that intelligent, warm, discreet man, Joseph Strauss the Berliner, and of his miraculous tea, which inspired dreams and indolence. At around midnight, however, he was informed by an officer that the dentist was not to be found.

Then, toward morning, he heard a murmuring brook and rustling grass; he saw a sunlit glade, with beeches, alders, and sycamores. He awoke bewildered and wet, and the stain on the sheets resembled neither spittle nor dried blood—it was different from other stains.

4 ✣ The Dwarf on the Tightrope

THE CANDLES HAD been snuffed out a short time before, and so in the rustling air only the gray soles of a pair of feet could be made out. When the darkness had diluted, the calves and thighs became visible, bared, tensed, sometimes entwined, then quickly unclenching. In the narrow bed, where the sheets smelled of lavender, two legs were slowly rocking, and another two were arching above them, trying to touch (the ankles, the heels), flexing back and then lifting towards the ceiling, as if they wanted to scrape the grainy whitewash. The rocking intensified, the broad motions became short jerks, the rustling air in the room ceased to rustle and was pervaded by heavy panting, by a faint whining and a groaning that burgeoned. The sheet slid from the hips, and amid the shadows of night a white bottom loomed, writhing wildly, up and down, back and forth. Then exhaustion descended, the beard no longer scratched against the plump bosom, it sank into its softness, the breathing settled into a normal cadence, moist lips twitched, a hand rested on a thigh, long, straight hair lay fanned out. Moments, plentiful moments, elapsed in this way, indolently, until the bodies separated and each lay stretched on its back, close together, giving off a warm mist. And in that mist, a small snub nose rediscovered the perfume it had forgotten for long minutes, a fine perfume of almond flowers, such as it had never encountered before, and another nose, hooked and prominent, sensed once more the lavender beneath the sheets, but paid it no heed and avid, astonished, and insatiable, it feasted on the moist odors of the woman's body. In his belly, something bunched up like a hedgehog and saddened when she propped herself on her elbow, rose (her right hand grasping the back of a chair and her left groping over the floor), took three steps, fumbled for the tin basin, the bucket of water, and the soap, washed long and thoroughly, calmly and languidly, dried herself likewise, at leisure, and drove away, at least for a time, the scent between her thighs, neither sweet nor bitter. The woman's palms settled, one on his shoulder, the other on his belly, they set out feeling and searching, they discovered the calfskin sheath with the drawstring at the mouth and the thread encrusted around it, they slowly removed it, like a scabbard, and immersed it in an infusion of sage, to cleanse it and keep it supple. Careful fingers grasped the tired, sticky phallus, bathed it, coddled it, caressed it like a babe, and as they could not give it suck, they allowed the breasts to embrace it and rock it. The man decided to light a cigar and uncork the champagne. He found neither an ashtray nor glasses, so he fetched a dish and some earthenware mugs. And in the iridescent darkness, the cork popped like a discharging pistol, it stirred up the dogs far and wide, it frightened the mice in the crannies and under the floorboards, it wakened the geese, and, far worse, provoked in the girl a dreadful shriek, followed by a leap as far as the table. He knelt on the jute mat, tousling her hair, he spoke to her continuously in French, he kissed her on the coccyx, on each rib and on her warm nape, his kisses made their way back to her soft, downy bottom, like a peach, but the kisses were no longer kisses, for he was already running the tip of his tongue down her spine, without giving the cigar or the champagne another thought. He descended lightheaded, smoothly, and he would have descended yet lower had she not twisted away. They stretched out once more on the narrow bed, propped against pillows and the wooden frame, they drank from the mugs without handles, then she moistened each of her nipples in the cold, fizzy liquid, gave them to him, and waited. It was a long time before her hands once more set out on their search. They found his member (which she petted with words such as he had never heard before: *pulicică, sulac, coinac,* and *ștremeleag*), thrust it into the mug, and they played with it, pampered it, scrubbed its tangled curls and rosy, childish head, and her lips wiped it well after its bath. Then the hands dressed it in its little kidskin coat, velvety and moist, they tightened the drawstring, and once more lost themselves in madness.

A king is a king, even if he is called *domn* or *domnitor,* but above all, a king is a man, because no one has ever been born on a throne or with a crown on his head. And he, Carol I, after ignoring the laws of nature and the needs of the body for more than a year, three hundred and eighty-four days, to be exact, always monopolized by and caught up in the convoluted problems of the Principalities, by the languor, by the chaotic commotion and urgent business around him, had avoided treading the slippery path of seamy liaisons. The end of spring found him gloomy and irascible, incapable of taking delight in the warm breezes, the peonies, and the cherry blossoms. Nor was his brother Friedrich, who had accompanied him during a long sojourn in Jassy and on a visit to the Danube ports, capable of brightening his mood. It was also around then that he received the news that his youngest sister, Marie, was to be engaged to the Count of Flanders, news that gave him a start, in the shadow of which, had it not been for his beard and bushy eyebrows, a crooked smile might have been deciphered. He wrote without delay, mimicking joy, but in the letters, commas, periods, and exclamation marks, as if the ink itself consisted of astonishment and regrets, he saw only the irony of fate. The man who had refused the rickety and uncomfortable throne upon which Carol himself now sat, that very man, the one with the eight Christian names, Philippe, Eugène, Ferdinand, Marie, Clément, Baudouin, Leopold, and George, happy and carefree in his castle in Laeken, near Brüssel, was to receive the gifts of the hand, the laughter, and the wonderfulness of his sister, the creature whom he, far away at the ends of the earth (as many believed), missed most of all, while he strove to restore to health a strange land whose people did not wish to rid themselves of their ailments. On the third of the month, in the afternoon, Prince Karl gazed absently at the foliage in front of his window, indifferent to the preparations for the May 10 festivities, inclined to see only hypocrisy and operatic gestures in that collective eagerness to celebrate the lapse of one year since his arrival in Bukarest. As so often before, he thought of the miraculous infusion he had drunk in Istanbul, before being received by the sultan, and he desired a teacupful, enough for him to forget what was gnawing away at him and to be happy for a few hours. He sent for Joseph Strauss, with the specific information that he was expecting a cup of tea, but he doubted from the outset that he would get what he demanded. He had not summoned him since March, after he had been obliged to appoint Kretzulescu to the head of the council of ministers, given Ghika's weariness of politics, and after he had corrected the draft of a law whereby a new currency, with the rather comical name *leul* ("the lion"), was to replace piasters, francs, and all the other foreign coins in circulation. And, indeed, on the third of the month, as afternoon drew toward dusk, the dentist appeared with his calfskin bag, ready to explain why he would not prepare an infusion of *Amanita muscaria, Fliegenpilz,* snake's hat, or snake mushroom. As he stood by the door, Herr Strauss strung together his protective and sorrowful lies. He said that the powder had run out in Constantinople, that he did not know with what herbs it had been made, that he had been given the desiccated preparation in Berlin by a traveling apothecary who had vanished without trace, that he, too, longed for the enchanted potion. The prince listened to him carefully, with that attitude of his which passed as stern and distant. He understood what was to be understood, because he held the conviction that to a man in whom you have no doubts you should grant, when required, the right to concoct a story. He invited him to sit on the couch of yellowish velvet, he sat down beside him, and they clinked glasses of tart white wine. They sat in silence. The tree by the window swayed softly, a plane tree with large, young leaves. Then Joseph, with his chin resting on his palms and his elbows resting on his knees, gazing at the waxed parquet, banished shame (because at that moment, perhaps because of the wine, his loyalty and affection were greater), and asked him. And the prince, appreciating the tone of his question, replied, with his eyes fixed on the ceiling: No. No, he had not touched a woman for a long time, not since he had donned the uniform of a captain of dragoons.

A week later, the tenth day of May 1867 dissolved differently from other days, with a gilded service at the Metropolia (for gilded were the robes of the Metropolitan Nifon, of the bishops and the priests of the great conclave), a reception laid on by the prince in the throne room (where he had delivered his first speech in Romanian, although his words, thanks to Professor Treboniu Laurian, had not much resembled those used by his subjects, having Latin forms and sounds) and a military parade down Podul Mogoşoaiei, which drew half the city to the avenue's sidewalks and excited three-quarters of the women. Later, while in the city hall new streets and boulevards were taking shape beneath the architects' nibs and on other large sheets of paper a new channel for the sluggish and stinking Dîmbovitza was being traced out, so that the river would no longer flood the city, the dentist was busy making sure that a small old reed-clad building near the Silvestru Church looked more like a home than a brothel. He had chatted and haggled long with an old madam named Mareta, flustering her with the tale of a rich client, a Dutch merchant with a predilection for blind whores, he had thrust into her palm a gold coin, a gulden, and finally he brought in some painters to whitewash the house front, the hall, and the rooms. The old woman and two of her girls scrubbed the floorboards and the woodwork, filled a mattress with fresh straw, shook out the pillows and aired them in the sun, washed the rugs, the sheets, the curtains, the coverlet, the tablecloth, and the wall hangings in the freshly whitewashed room, rinsing them repeatedly with lavender, placed new candles in the earthenware candlesticks, arranged mugs and plates on a shelf, stowed the chamber pot and a basin under the bed, laid clean towels over the back of the chair, placed a tablet of soap on the edge of the stove, readied a glass jug, and did not hurry to cut flowers then; rather, they waited until noon on the sixteenth day of May, when they knew it was time, and picked lilies and roses in the yard. First, two carts arrived in the lane, sent by that pale, thin German, and gravel was laid along the path from the gate up to the porch. The third girl, Linca, had not taken any part in the labor, so as not to spoil her hands and her stamina. Mareta gave her a long bath, as if she were soaking laundry. She rubbed her with ass's milk and strawberries, combed her hair and sprinkled it with rose-hip oil, and when ruddy evening fell, when the artisans' quarter resounded to the lowing and bleating before milking, gave her a teaspoonful of honey in which she had sprinkled a little powdered stag-beetle horn. Meanwhile, in the center of Bucuresci, a man in the twenty-ninth year of his life, a man who found himself in the office of the sovereign, sitting in the chair of the sovereign's desk, took it into his head to cut his fingernails. And as it was none other than he, Karl Eitel Friedrich Zephyrinus Ludwig, sitting in that chair, in that office, in that palace, and since he was the sovereign of a land about to embark upon summer with ripening fields of wheat and awakening clouds of dust, he asked his ministers and those on the audience list for a breathing space of two minutes. Using a silver-plated pair of clippers, he trimmed his fingernails as short as possible, then meticulously gathered them and sprinkled them in the wastepaper basket, waiting to stroke the unknown skin with his fingertips and surrender himself to tactile sensation.

In the silence of sleep and night, when an owl might have hooted, but did not hoot, a short man in the garb of a Western merchant or ship owner, with the hood of his cape pulled up to shield against damp, mosquitoes, and miasmas, passed by a soldier of the guard, without waking him, and went out by a back door. He climbed into a carriage, an ordinary one, and shook the hand of the man therein, who was wearing a cloak and a hat with a curved brim. They looked into each other's eyes as they left the palace grounds together, amid a clatter of horses' hooves, skirted the Bucureştioara, a stagnant, marshy stream, bumped along potholed narrow streets that smelled of jasmine and cesspits, of chicken coops and lilac; and came to a stop in the darkness. The passengers entered a spacious yard and walked down a graveled path. On the porch, the shorter man removed his hood and remained alone as the other man departed, after making sure once more that the area was deserted.

The fingertips had reached the point of torpor some time after midnight, a few hours still before the frail light of dawn. And together with the fingertips, the bodies had given themselves up to a long abandonment, like two huge seashells, buried in a straw mattress rather than the sands of an estuary. That torpor was disturbed, all of a sudden, by a sneeze. Then came more sneezes, muffled at first, then loud and irritating, one after another and seemingly uncontrollable. Murkily, the man remembered war maneuvers of long ago, when as a junker or cadet he had sheltered in hay ricks, stables, and attics, and a military doctor, a major, had warned him that he was allergic to hay. He got out of bed, naked, drank some champagne straight from the bottle, blew his nose loudly, left the handkerchief on the table, and held his breath for almost a minute, pinching his nostrils and ears so that no air would enter. The girl was saying something, she felt sorry for him and she was afraid, but he spoke to her in German, feigning not to understand her. He sat on the chair, blinking to get rid of the droplets that were trickling between his eyelashes. Soon, he felt her hands on his ankles, they climbed his calves and knees, rested for a moment and then glided down to the soles of his feet, they grasped his big toes, squeezing them gently, slowly, they ascended once more, sliding their way over his thighs and upward. In the gray light, he could distinguish only the crown of her head, her shoulders, and breasts, and for a few moments he wanted also to see her face, to caress it, but he forgot this desire. The hands moved higher and gripped his buttocks, allowing the small, gentle head to find room between his legs, under his belly. He tousled her long, straight hair, first spreading it like a fan or a peacock's tail, then parting it in the middle and laying it over her arms, to the left and right, chestnut-colored and silky, like two wings. From beneath her locks there came warm breaths, fleeting touches, peace. All of a sudden, the low room was no longer a room, the darkness was no longer darkness, the convoluted problems of the Principalities crumbled to dust, the maps of the continent shed their colors and contours, they whitened like cream, the seasons merged along with sun and azure sky into the gallop of a gray pony over a boundless plain, bearing in its saddle a little boy, Karl Ludwig, who loved his wooden targets—the hares, boars, and foxes—and did not want to riddle them with pellets. The little boy was carrying in the breast pocket of his tunic a lead soldier, and the man was clasping the nape of a young woman with his fingertips, as her mouth opened wide and moist.

When the Dutch merchant went out the front door, after the second cockcrow, it was impossible for the girl to see his profile (aquiline according to some), but she touched an unfamiliar object on the table, she stroked the delicate cloth and clenched it in her fist. It was his handkerchief, with a monogram.

Siegfried was in the wicker basket. In the other basket, made of osier, there was a jug of milk, some fried fish, half a chicken breast, and some sweet cheese. The first basket hung as ever from the arm of Joseph Strauss, and the high, curved handle of the second was in the hands of Otto Huer. They advanced with difficulty, in the middle of February, when the cold sometimes bore the name of frost and warmer days still seemed distant. On that Sunday the cobblestones were cracking beneath the white expanse that had blanketed garbage, horse flop, potholes, gutters, rat tunnels, molehills, and carrion. At a crossroads, the dentist had almost stumbled over a dead sorrel horse, whose chest, furrowed by ribs, was poking through the snow. They were heading toward the Batiştei quarter, in search of the house of the washerwoman Leana, who every Saturday collected the towels, cotton napkins, and smocks from Otto's shop, returning them clean and ironed on Mondays. They found the house easily by asking a group of urchins gathered around some curled-up, shivering dogs on a patch of waste ground. A young man nearby, wrapped up snugly in a felt coat, discovered the tomcat in the basket, blew out his snots, and laughed. They had never heard of two gentlemen in German garb paying a visit to a she-cat. Leana showed them inside and offered them pumpkin pies. The young man showed them a jug of apricot brandy and some copper beakers, and the urchins showed them the she-cat. And after they had all stared their fill, Siegfried, the real guest, jumped from the basket. Ritza sniffed him from afar, tensed, she lifted up her tail, paced slowly, inquisitively forward, sensed something, bristled her whiskers and approached, then she sensed more things and all of a sudden flung herself down on the bare earth that served instead of floorboards, with her paws outstretched and her head held back. She was meowing softly. Then she twisted around and meowed sharply. The two of them, Siegfried and Manastamirflorinda, touched noses, they rubbed up against each other and against all the things around, they sang their duet (and those people, like all people, thought they were purring), and at last, while their tails in passing entwined (hers black, with a ruddy spot at the tip, his white, with a black tuft), from the trapdoor of the attic, through a little hole, there emerged four kittens. They paused on the top steps of the ladder that leaned against the wall. They hissed and spat at the unfamiliar tomcat. They descended slowly, fearfully, hesitantly, nudged forward by their mother, who had stopped calling them and climbed up to them with agile bounds. Then, as Joseph and Otto munched hot pies and the beakers had once more been filled with apricot brandy, it happened that the two tomcats came face to face, one large and imperturbable, the other small and bellicose, always on the prowl, lurking and growling, the fur on his nape bristling, his ears pricked up, his back arched and his tail puffed up like a shaving brush. They looked so much alike that the dentist, tossing back the brandy, had the feeling that the present Siegfried was being menaced by the former Siegfried, as he had been three years previously, when Joseph found him in the Gendarmeriemarkt under a blossoming acacia bush. And the tomcat moved once, as swift as an arrow, placing his paw on the top of the kitten's head, he stopped him fighting, licked him, and lulled him. He did the same with his sisters, little lumps of fur that were tabby like Manastamirflorinda and pressed trembling against her belly. Later, he jumped up onto the table, searched in the osier basket, and grasped a piece of perch with his teeth. The kittens tore at it from four directions, seized by passion, bravery, and hunger. By the time Siegfried thrust the chicken meat toward them, they seemed exhausted and full. Smoking his pipe, Joseph read the countless lines on the face of the woman and gazed into the wide eyes of the children. He put on his overcoat, scarf, cap, and gloves in silence, whispered something to the barber, and left. He returned in less than an hour to find the kittens asleep, curled up among the bones of the chicken breast. He placed a canvas bag on the table, and extracted from therein everything he had been able to find in the larder at home: sausages, honey, olives, salted cheese, ham, smoked fish, bonbons, and wine. He also gave them a silver coin, to purchase the cats. Then the dentist and the barber departed through the creaking snow with the tomcat in the wicker basket, the she-cat in the osier basket, and the kittens in the canvas bag, wrapped up in an old sweater. At the midway point between Saturday and Monday, Otto Huer had seen for the first time what became of his laundry in that interval. At lunchtime, the smocks were lying in a long trough to soak, and the towels and napkins were hanging on lines to dry around the oven. He knew that for a long time he would not be rid of the annoying feeling that his linen was imbued with a stale reek of pies and brandy.

Amid the deafening din of the Whitsuntide fair in June of that year, Joseph Strauss was not engrossed in buying calves, cattle, mules, guinea fowl, or other poultry. He wanted to see the city at play in the early summer, when the light blended with poplar down and swarms of flies. And it blended in greenish ways, as pale as a duck's egg, as wan as willow leaves, as murky as stewed nettles, depending on how the sun pierced through the clouds. That morning, walking and standing, but mostly walking, he could distinguish these three shades, especially after he left the sprawling market with its throng of horse traders and peddlers, cattle dealers and water carriers, bookkeepers and servants, shepherds and pickpockets, boyars and paupers, people of many nations and places, heated, high-spirited, seeking bargains, flowing between the herds of horses and cattle, the flocks of sheep and goats. It was a murmuring throng above which floated the cries of the animals, as if at the edge of Bucuresci the Tower of Babel and Noah's Ark had merged. He made his way toward one of the exits and cooled off with a sheep's milk yogurt, sour and cold, and to give himself more time to catch his breath, he bought not baklava, or gingerbread, or pistachios, but the one thing he most desired as the sun's disk sparkled and the light dissolved like linden tea trickling into a pail of water: roast chestnuts. Then he made his way southward, cracking the shells with his fingernails and his teeth, munching the kernels, crushing them with the tip of his tongue and swallowing the milky pulp a little at a time. He walked slowly, so as to be able to observe at leisure, to feel, and to discover. He walked around mountains of crockery, sizzling grills, heaps of tablecloths and carpets, pie sellers, piles of spoons, spindles, and rolling pins, kvass sellers, palm readers, fortune tellers (and among them a large-bosomed woman who read the future with her left breast), he strolled amid saucepans, kettles, pots, and alembics, amid barrels, casks, and tubs, he listened to gypsy fiddlers (unable to tear his eyes from a thick-lipped fiddler beating time with his wooden leg), at a toy stall he picked out for Siegfried a black wooden mouse (in whose belly was concealed a spool of thread and a spring), he passed by mounds built from balls of wool, bundles of frieze, and bolts of linen, by the stalls of tanners and skinners, by the shelves of cobblers, by the hundreds and hundreds of tailor's racks, by the vendors of candles, lamps, mirrors, boxes, harnesses, and wicks, he looked all around him, and even up and down, at the trampled ground and at the patches of clear sky, he discovered and examined many things and once again he grew thirsty, so thirsty that he thought even the beer teemed with the same green glints as the light of the day. He drained two mugs, tossing back the first, sipping the second, letting the fizzy liquid slip soothingly down his throat. And then he penetrated to the heart of the fair, wandering for hours on end. His walk was an undulating line, and the undulating line was the track of a lazy snake, a snaking that was inevitable, an inevitability called fate. Herr Strauss could not be distinguished among the motley mob, but he was there as it was proper for him to be, so as not to upset the logic of things and so as to fulfill events, all the events of that late spring of the year, 1868. Beneath a bunch of sunbeams as fine as pondweed, he glimpsed a profile with rosy cheeks, flushing or confused, with curly locks poking from under a hat, touching the left earlobe, with a small chin that resembled a ripe apricot. He quivered, hoping and believing that it was Mathilde Vogel, and in that tremulous state he wondered, as he had in the yard of the Catholic Church some time ago, whether it was worth approaching her, whether the fine sunbeams gladdened her or saddened her, whether her strappy shoes pinched, whether her thighs were smooth and moist. He wondered without moving, until the quivering died away, and then he remembered that the optician's sister had become engaged before Lent and that he himself had attended the lively engagement party. Mathilde was to be wedded to Schütze the notary, a Calvinist, and the distant profile proved to be that of another woman, who was waving a cherry-red fan and who turned toward him, revealing how deceptive is the countenance of the weaker sex. He smiled. Then he had a smoke. And he smiled once more at the antics and the capers of some clowns, he grew dizzy on a carousel turned by four donkeys, he quickly grew bored of juggled balls, torches, and skittles, he laughed heartily at a puppet show, in which Vasilache and Mărioara tussled on a tiny stage (a crate with the bottom knocked out and set on its side, with a crêpe skirt for a curtain), he watched the dancing bears with rings through their snouts, and was filled with pity, he nibbled walnuts roasted in salt, he fired a bow and arrow, ineptly, at the pear on a scarecrow's head (and did not win the prize of a demijohn of plum brandy), he applauded the brass bands and vaudeville acts, he gave spinning tops and lollipops to Peter Bykow's freckled boys (hand in hand with their father), he bet with the baker on the wrestling bouts, but kept losing, they toasted each other with a mug of sweet red wine and parted, and Joseph threw his head back to catch a view of three acrobats perched each on the other's shoulders, he met an old man on stilts and a one-legged man riding a boar (a stuffed boar, maneuvered with strings and levers from behind a curtain), he shuddered for the dwarf who was prancing and leaping on a tightrope stretched between two posts. After he finished his balancing act and acrobatics, the dwarf collected a few coins in a copper cup, but as he drew closer to Joseph he somehow also seemed to grow longer. Through the greenish-blond strands of sunlight, the dentist saw the dwarf's arms and legs extending, his body becoming fuller, his head, as his proportions shifted, no longer looked like a pumpkin, his strides became long and smooth, and his striped trousers, red waistcoat, and high-soled shoes grew with him. The dwarf who was no longer a dwarf offered Joseph a scarf and asked him to blindfold himself, and he consented, allowing himself to be led through the din of the fair. Finally, they reached a shady, quiet place, like a cool cellar, although they had not descended any steps, and Herr Strauss undid the knot of the scarf. The dwarf who was no longer a dwarf scrutinized Joseph and meanwhile continued to elongate, inch by inch. And he told him that the gates of the heavens would soon open, not to unleash whirlwinds, floods, and devastation, but to reveal a pale, bluish flame, like burning ethanol, within which he would glimpse things such as he had never experienced and times with a different taste. Joseph wanted to question him, to hear details, but suddenly he woke up in a sweat, with his shoulder leaning against a tree and a handkerchief in his left hand, as if he had swooned briefly in the bustle of the late morning. He quickly came to after a glass of kvass, the apparition faded from his mind, and lured once more by the rustling dresses and the gentle breeze, he entered the tents that loomed in his path, paying as before a few coppers and finding within all kinds of oddities, though none like the one in his dream. He saw a hunchback puffing on eight pipes, without any of them going out, a young woman in shalwars and a turban, knitting, with her ankles crossed behind her neck, a blindfolded knife thrower maiming fearsome wolves painted on a panel made of planks, an incomparable fat lady beneath a gauzy veil, through which could be glimpsed her immensity, a gypsy who turned a sandglass and then immersed himself in a tub of water (until all the sand had drained through), a redheaded woman with a beard down to her chest, knotted in pigtails so as not to cover her breasts, rat fights in a glass vessel (the slaughter transparent), shadow plays cast against a white sheet by clever fingers moving in front of a candle, a long-haired man treading barefoot over broken glass and nails, a huge penis, two feet long, preserved in a jar of formaldehyde, magicians, belly dancers, fire-eaters, a crocodile, seemingly asleep, storytellers, and much more. After so many follies seen and heard, he felt as if his head had swollen to twice its size, though it looked the same as always: a little tapered, with wavy chestnut hair and pale skin. At the southern edge of the fair, he stopped at the booth of an itinerant innkeeper and ordered a cutlet and some greens. He was spent. He sat, extending his long, skinny legs under the table as far as they would stretch. Slowly, the flurry of devilish images in his mind faded away. He had just gulped down a huge, gristly mouthful when someone tapped him on the back of the neck and uttered his name. Spluttering, he turned around and saw Carol, not the prince, but another man.

This particular Carol wore a frock coat with broad lapels, a striped waistcoat, a white shirt, a beard trimmed so that the edge was round, like a collar, and boots with two rows of buckles. His eyes were bulbous and lacked lashes, his hair was combed back, his lips were cracked. All in all, his features made him look like a plump thrush. He remained on his feet, filling the minutes with dry observations about the whirlwinds of dust that would soon whip up, about the dog-day heat that stalked the horizon, about the fleeting summer rains. He did not sit down until mugs of beer fringed with thick creamy foam appeared and he grasped one by the handle and glued it to his mouth until he had emptied it. For a little while, he exhaled greenish, sluggish vapors, which enveloped him and then dissolved. They were sitting on a narrow bench near the main gate, whose ivy and roses brought to mind a pergola for promenading ladies and gentlemen. They had not talked together for a good few weeks, not since before the last snowfall, a storm that had loomed over the council of ministers held after Prince Karl Ludwig's twenty-ninth birthday and after he had yet again been driven to the limit of his patience, a late and feeble spring snowstorm, which turned into a breeze and a family affair, with Zinca Golescu's older son, Ştefan, being replaced as head of government by her younger son, Nicolae, the general and former triumvir. Many things had taken place since their last meeting, and the newcomer lingered to sip cold, tongue-tingling beer and tell his tales. He had lived in Bucuresci for a quarter of a century, and besides knowing all the well to do, all the full purses, he also knew the city's history. And as the poplar fluff and midges floated by, he told the dentist that in the past hangings had been carried out in that very spot where they now quenched their thirst, after the condemned were marched there in chains, being whipped as they went, as a lesson for the commoners and as an opportunity for *chiloman* and jibes. And after the gibbets in the reign of Brîncoveanu, he went on, under Mavrocordat they erected stakes at the Moşilor tollgate on which they impaled *calpuzani* in the winter, to set the merchants' minds at rest and slake the mob's thirst for executions. At those unfamiliar words, *chiloman* and *calpuzani*, Joseph raised his eyebrows in incomprehension, and that other Carol decided to relinquish Romanian, and explained in fluent German, but with a Cluj accent, that he had been talking about the fever of the mob and counterfeiters, respectively. They went on drinking and seldom looked at each other, rather, they gazed over each other's head at the horizon, one to the north, the other to the south, deciphering the various glints of the afternoon, the streaks like bean pods at one edge of the heavens and a fine, slightly verdigris dust at the other bourn. Since his nocturnal visit to the Silvestru quarter thirteen months earlier, Herr Strauss had been summoned to the palace only once, for a recalcitrant canine with inflamed roots, and so he wanted to find out more about Karl Eitel Friedrich Zephyrinus Ludwig, a man extraordinarily dear to him, a man whom he missed. With his arms folded across his chest, he listened to the voice of the watercolorist, a drawling voice that frequently accompanied the prince on his travels around the country and in the past had kept four other rulers company—

Ghika, Bibescu, Ştirbei, and Cuza—and that could often be heard in the mansarded studio at the top of the Green Inn, where the voice's owner made daguerreotypes, talbotypes, and stereotype plates, some with a coating of albumin and silver iodide, others with wet collodion. From that plump thrush of a man there gradually flowed news and details: about the prince's skill in reading his subjects, about the fury that their indolence and toadying aroused in him, about his impeccable general's uniform with its gold epaulettes, about the establishment of a new sort of academy, christened the Literary Society, about his inspections of barracks, grain silos, railways, and ports, about his weakness for miniatures, portraits, and landscapes unsullied by Impressionism, about the purchase of two artillery batteries from Krupp and twenty thousand rifles, about his numerous excursions to the country, including one on horseback through the enchanted forest of the Peleş Valley. Their chat was suddenly interrupted—somewhere beyond the gate, a commotion had broken out. Couples walking arm in arm quickened their pace, a throng of expensive attire (silk gloves, canes, lorgnettes, hats, handbags, medals, high-heeled shoes, voilettes, buttonholes, jewels, and *lavallières*) amid which excited exclamations could be made out. The crowd was flocking toward a marble tower in the middle of the fairground. The other Carol stood up, inclined his head, and left at a run, coming to a halt next to an extraordinary apparatus on whose sides was inscribed *Painter and Photographer to H. M. the Prince*. And as he ran he oscillated between his real name, Carol Popp de Szathmari, and that demanded by fashion and elegance, Charles Szathmáry. The dentist paid for the beers, cutlet, and greens, and then headed to the site of the impending event. He made his way through the crowd with difficulty, moving along its edge, viewing as if in a giant tableau the Bucuresci beau monde and the allegorical temple at its center, which proved to be made not of marble but lacquered stucco, a mixture of slaked lime, chalk dust, gelatin, and glue. It rested on a wooden plinth in the shape of a dodecagon, with railings and statuettes symbolizing the months of the year, and was girdled with garlands of lilies, daisies, and laurel leaves that climbed it in a spiral. At the pinnacle, above the whispers and manners of high society, there was a large bowl, also of stucco, shaped like a gigantic water lily, with six petals. While the procession of carriages was still some way off, near the area of the stalls, and Karl Ludwig was waving from the banquette of a white coach and bestowing upon the people some words in Romanian, the crowd of ladies and gentlemen parted in two (the same as one might part cream by running one's finger through the middle), without taking their eyes off the slowly advancing conveyances. Soon the horses reached the path that had opened between all those distinguished faces. They were snuffling, perhaps because of the perfumes and French phrases, perhaps because they had had enough of galloping, trotting, and mincing, and wanted their oats. From a small viewing tower, built especially for him and his apparatus, the watercolorist immortalized those moments, experimenting with panoramas, as he had sometimes done from the tops of Metropolia, Filaret, and the Spirii hills, from the Colţei Tower and the attic of the Grand Theatre. Joseph kept treading on people's toes, he was jostled and crushed by the curious onlookers, he was trying not to miss any of the prince's movements, to decipher whatever there was to be deciphered in the way the prince blinked, reacted to the bowing, deigned to laugh, or showed a serious mien, and above all in the way he smoothed his beard or sideburns, slowly with the index finger, or rapidly with all five. He could see only snatches, only fragments, and so he began to elbow his way forward torturously, striving to reach Szathmari's viewing tower. At the bottom of the ladder he clashed with a soldier of the guard and was shoved back with a rifle butt. However, he did not give up, but shouted at the top of his voice, drawing dozens of glances, and among them the one that mattered. The photographer descended and pacified the soldier, then scurried back up to the platform together with Herr Strauss. The still-young Carol I, second son of Prince Karl Anton, the former prime minister of Prussia and now, on that very Wednesday, military governor of Rhineland, and himself a former Prussian officer, a captain in the Berlin regimental guard, to be exact, seemed to be in his element and was chatting freely. It is hard to say whether the sovereign, besieged with cheers, bows, curtsies, and elegant attire, had time to contract the pupils of his eyes and scan the background. He might have been able to recognize, alongside the court photographer, the dentist with whom he had lost touch and about whom, sometimes, forgetting his embarrassment, he would have liked to hear news.

Two hours later, the light faded and took on a baleful potency, resembling the glow of putrid swamps or gloomy, witch-haunted woods, a whistle of angry, threatening light, as gusts of wind snatched away the garlands and wreaked havoc among the tents and stalls. The storm began suddenly. It shattered the repose of amorous glances, intrigues, backstabbing, and honeyed fawning. The cream of the nation was drenched, the vaporous gowns were deflated, the striped trousers were rumpled, the high-heeled and lacquered shoes were spattered with mud, the courtesies were transformed into an uproar of short feminine shrieks and irritated masculine shouts, a stampede toward the carriages and coupés, which in their turn were embroiled in a dreadful hullaballoo, hampered by one another and by all those confused and sopping people. Herr Strauss, shivering and holding his coat over his head, kept near the fence, hoping by some miracle to find shelter or a cab. In a corner on the eastern side of the grounds, as he was never to forget, he lifted his eyes to decide which way to go and met a pair of blue, warm, and haughty eyes that scrutinized him, eyes in which there was no fear. For a few seconds he did not move, who knows for how many, he did not feel the raindrops falling on his face or the water in his boots. He thought that shelter was to be found within those eyes, where happiness had taken refuge. When he came to his senses, he discovered that they belonged to a brown-haired woman with white skin and a slender neck and a little dimple in her chin, like the hollow of a shell. Her long locks were plastered to her cheeks, her clothes were sticking to her skin, and at her thighs pressed two young children, a boy and a girl, wrapped in a beige shawl and sheltered from the downpour by a parasol. At once, he threw his coat over her shoulders, then leaped in front of the first passing cab, his shirt fluttering, his feet planted in the greasy mud of the road, his arms raised. The cabman was about to strike him with his whip, but he reined in his horses, gazing at Joseph apprehensively. The svelte Lipizzaners came to a halt, champing at their bits. Joseph spoke to one of the passengers, shook the hand that was extended to him through the half-opened door, conducted the woman and children through the lashing rain, helped them to climb aboard, and then climbed aboard himself, thanking the good Lord and Judge Farmache, their saviors. It was not until they were within, all four huddled on one of the benches, for on the other were seated the magistrate and his wife, that he learned her name. It was a Serbian name. Beneath her blue eyes, as the horses raced over the Outer Market Bridge, her fleshy, slightly purple lips smiled at him. Bizarrely, although he might have been thinking about the Erdreich Baths, with their scorching steam and basins of hot water, all of a sudden he remembered his dream of the dwarf and that pale flame within which he had glimpsed so many things. The woman's eyes enveloped him. There was no need for other words.

Sometime in July, while blazing heat weighed on the city, another three chairs in the day room had their backrests slashed to ribbons. Herr Strauss was no longer surprised, he did not take it to heart, nor did he imagine that the velvet, full of gashes, rents, slits, and punctures, hundreds, perhaps thousands of them, had been gnawed by moths or pecked by sharp-beaked birds. The author of the textile carnage was Siegfried, there could be no doubt, but the deeds and the impulses of the tomcat were worth infinitely more to Joseph than the state of the upholstery. Besides, aflame during those days, not because of the heat but for reasons of amour, Joseph no longer saw the objects around him and often forgot to eat. He would go missing from home for long periods, he slept little and restlessly, and whenever he was to be found in the rooms of the upper story of the redbrick house, at number 18 Lipscani Lane, he would content himself with holding the tomcat in his lap, stroking him and talking to him. His thoughts would wander aimlessly, he would remember and conjure up places, gestures, pangs, touches, always beneath the glitter of blue Serbian eyes. One afternoon, on the feast of the prophet Elijah, in the darkened room he began to tell Siegfried what he had heard that very morning from her lips, in the courtyard of the Stavropoleos Inn, when the chiming of the bells had once more filled the sky. He translated into German for the cat how God's charioteer, flying in his car of fire and with

87

seven cannons to hand, could cast down upon sinners rain, drought, famine, cholera, plague, perdition, and war, how the prophet Elijah was the patron not only of cloudbursts but also of bees, and how on his feast day he caused the dead to wander abroad and honey to be harvested from the hives. The tomcat purred softly, with his black ear pricked up and the tip of his tail aloft, with his muzzle resting between his master's clavicles, and the chestnut-haired, thin man, looking thinner than ever, told him all that had been spoken to him, troubled less by the fury of the Apocalypse and more by the black wind-tousled hair, by the throat as slender as a new shoot, by the plump lobes of the ears, by the small dimple in the chin. As if with a mouth not his own he spoke about the blood that will gush forth and scorch the earth if the Unclean One manages to cut off the head of Saint Elijah, about the folk that will be born and resemble the Blazhini, the Meek Folk who live on the banks of the River at the Ends of the Earth, about the huge burial mound whence will emerge the souls of all the dead, incarnated as sheep and goats, the former following the Good Lord, the latter the Devil. He related calmly things that had been told to him with passion in her low, slightly singsong voice, in a Romanian full of slips (different errors than his own), a language mangled but enchanting in its way, because it bound him fast to Elena Duković. And, to conclude the nocturnal narrative, Herr Strauss poured himself a tumbler of raki and sweetened it with honey, throwing it back in the company of his best friend, the tomcat, since he had just learned that this is an Orthodox custom at the Feast of the Prophet, when the honeycombs overflow and the hives are moved. He did not care about the backrests of the chairs. Nor did he even recall that the first among them had been clawed during his voyage to Istanbul. Almost two years had passed since then, and on different occasions, Siegfried had written on the yellow velvet:

(on the middle chair along the side of the table by the stove)
Only you, good Otto Huer, enchanter, showed a warm heart in the dead of winter, you took pity and made me breathe quickly, more quickly than I have ever breathed before, I was suffocating and gulping the air with knots in my throat, like those athirst, for many things have happened, barber, countless things, firstly you scattered the mystery and yearning, you opened the eyes of my beloved master and made him turn his ear to your words, together you strode through the snowdrifts, and the cold and wind frightened you not, I know, you pressed that door handle, you, glorious one, may your scissors ever be sharp, you opened the door, you let the heat of the chamber lap over us and let us guess at the wonders within, I thought I would faint, lose myself, not because of the fire, but because of the ruddy flecks in her fur, Manastamirflorinda stepped forth shyly and with wonderment, she was quivering, again I heard how you called her Ritza and I tried to soothe her shame, to steal it away, to scatter it, love brooks no insistent stares, O barber, and time flowed slowly until she purred, it took some moments, and the moments were long, my breast was fit to burst, I was crawling with unseen ants, happiness has a tart taste, I tell you, her moist nose touched me and her tail spoke to me, it is a secret, I shall not divulge it, not her eyes but the moments gleamed, you humans think that cats purr, and all of a sudden the heavens seeped through the ceiling and the ceiling washed over us, I was rid of the ants, you did not drink and you did not eat, from the swirling white heavens and from the cloudlike ceiling what dripped

was not tears, not snowflakes, but four droplet-like kittens,
I wanted to cry out, but my mouth would not obey me, I
wanted to flee, but my legs were limp, I wanted to taste the
milk from her dugs, but Manastamirflorinda had become one
with my children, I grew dizzy and leaned against the wall,
dear one, you must understand, the world is much more than
we suspect, the spots in her fur were ruddy flecks of sun, you
both laughed and believed that she-cats purr, the scent of the
hot pie and the steam of the boiled brandy wafted over us, and
the miracle did not spring from a mirror in which I saw my
own face, it was not a phantasm, not a dream, the valiant
tomcat with his hackles up looked just like me, but smaller, I
thought I would faint, lose myself, that I would take flight,
and to thee, to thee only, dear Otto Huer, I now confess that
on the way back, when you and my beloved master set off
once more through the snows and chill wind, verily did I take
flight, in my mind, alongside Manastamirflorinda, in my
wicker basket, with my muzzle buried in her belly. Thanks
be to thee, good Otto, be thou protected and may thy razor cut
deftly!

(on the chair in the corner by the window)
How all things mingle, master, wonderful master! How
close is sweet to bitter and how swiftly light is changed to
darkness, I thought that goodness had been poured upon this
house, that nothing and no one could drive it out, I bathed
at ease in the water of joy after you gave me the greatest, the
most bewildering gift, after you, gentle Joseph, angel, allowed
another five feline souls into your chambers, after you smiled
and puffed on long curved pipes, you kept watch over us in
your armchair as though from the boundless azure heavens,
and we melted, six bodies, twelve ears, twenty-four paws,

singing, not purring, we rolled together in a lazy tabby ball,
on the rugs or under the dresser with five drawers, a ball with
spots of ruddy fur, softly crackling, like hot coals, as though
happiness were eternal, a ball from which sometimes rose a
fluffed-up white tail with a black tuft at the tip, a wee tail
like a flower stalk, so deceptive, master, but it let me imagine
harmony does not perish, a wee tail that one fine morning of
gray clouds all of a sudden went limp and trembled, together
with the other three wee tails, with their gleaming points of
flame, my children were first of all astonished, they made to
fondle their mother and imitate the lullabies of her throat,
they were cadging milk, of course, from her firm, swollen dugs,
but they were met with frowns, with blows, with unfamiliar
growls, Manastamirflorinda, my heart, leaped on top of the
tall cupboard, where the dust reigns and the swirling smoke
collects, I caressed her in my mind, from afar, and only then
did I decipher her looks, I swear to you, two looks, because
the green of her eyes had been sundered into rival halves,
one with vernal meadows full of gophers, the other new and
steely, threatening, I shuddered and again I fell in love, do not
laugh, Joseph Strauss, my friend, I felt in that moment how
the end began, I saw how her soul wandered, perhaps you,
too, saw it or perhaps you were lighting your black, healing
pipe, I heard the soft steps of the coming storm, creeping
closer, I was not afraid, but I grew sad, the hours ticked by
differently and time grew damp, then I glimpsed streaks of
lightning beyond the walls and windows, beyond the houses
and fields, I heard the muffled thunderclaps, out of nowhere,
the tempest broke upon us, dear one, and Manastamirflorinda
changed her care for the kittens into enmity and anger, she
chased them from her dugs, you humans say that she-cats
purr, and likewise you say that they spit, the truth is in

hymns and hate, it was necessary for you, big-hearted and
tender one, to seek welcoming homes for my children, to give
me leave to wash and fondle them, one by one, on parting,
you let me accompany them, you, Joseph, to convince me that
they would fall into good hands, there were four journeys and
on each something shattered within me, I will not conceal
from you that I wept for my matchless he-kitten, a red-hot
iron burnt me, him I shall never forget because there are
mirrors aplenty in the world, I shall not lie to you, dear one,
be at peace, memory is short and the wounds soon closed,
Manastamirflorinda descended to the rugs and bandaged
them, her little tongue, like a petal, licked my scars, I grew
drunk, I was dead drunk without sipping your aromatic
schnapps, you were away from home a long time, long enough
for us to be alone amid rustlings, caresses, and passions, you
wandered the whole night long, long enough for us to be
convinced that we were enveloped in dense, impenetrable
vapors, until the two of you, a dentist and a barber, entered
those steamy chambers, and Otto Huer, incomparable
enchanter, clapped his palms and caused Manastamirflorinda
all at once to have a master, he struck the floor with the sole of
his shoe and that master was he, a blessed barber, so that we,
loving thee, she and I, might meet often and ever meow.

(on a chair in another corner, the nearest)
You are withering away, day after day, dear one, you scorch
and burn yourself, your cheeks have grown blue and you have
deep bags under your eyes, you, Joseph, how much longer will
you torture yourself? You do not understand my language
and my pleas fall on deaf ears, I am not the one chosen to
give counsel, I have decided to keep my silence, I merely sing,

*ceaselessly, even if sometimes you forget that I exist, in your
lap it is warm and peaceful, on your breast it is like an island
with grasses and plump mice, you speak so much, untiringly,
you do not grow hoarse, lately I can no longer follow you,
the words slide away, collide with the windows and vanish,
where do they vanish? Why do they vanish? It is a mystery
and the mysteries are not unraveled for me, the hardest for me
is listening to the tumult in your heart, the tempest, as though
two armies were clashing, who is at war? Why so many cries?
Why such grim fury? These are the battles of love, I know,
and ashamed I make bold to think of them, but how can I
avoid it, dear one, how can I flee? Your body has weakened
and your deeds slumber, you seem powerless or bewitched,
I know you, goodly Joseph, as none other knows you and I
worship you like the sun, any knife that thrusts into your body
stabs me too, what pains you pains me, you are a dentist and
the gnashing of your teeth gives me shivers, I want to hide
and to endure it, I touch your hands and feet with my muzzle,
my whiskers have guessed that you have wings, love has given
you wings, my friend, and you needs must soar into the air, a
woman awaits you, I want to see you gliding, now I am alone
and desolate, you will return late, you will tell me your tales,
you will tremble and perspire, I am not hungry, or thirsty,
I am not at all sleepy, nor will you eat, you will not drink
and you will not sleep, I know, you will tell your dreams
aloud, sighing you will hope, your fingers will briefly stretch,
indifferent, then they will clench into a fist, inestimable Joseph
Strauss, healer, how much would I like to heal thee and to
promise thee that thy bitter minutes, hours, and days will
pass, that the second will arrive, one among all, when thou
wilt hold in thy palms her life and her soul.*

This much and thus wrote Siegfried on the yellow velvet, over twenty-two months during which the unpausing calendars measured the century and his claws were desirous to scratch. Of the six chairs, only two remained unscathed, indulgently receiving the shadows of twilight on the evening of the feast of Saint Elijah, as the stifling heat dissipated and through open windows could be heard far-off barking, raised voices, and, softly, very softly, the squeaks of bats emerging from attics. The dentist had shed his jacket and shirt by the side of the bed, he was stuffing tobacco into one of his pipes and striving with all his might to forget that in the kitchen, hidden in a flacon swaddled in cloth, placed in its turn in a well-stoppered jar (and the jar placed in a box bound with string, behind other boxes, behind sacks of lentils, flour, coarse sugar, buckwheat, beans, pearl barley, and oats, on the highest shelf in the larder), could be found that miraculous powder of *Amanita muscaria*, which had the power to wipe away many evils, bringing in their stead peace and joy. He smoked and did not manage to forget.

5 ✤ Footwear for Dolls

ELENA DUKOVIĆ HAD small hands and slender wrists, and when she alighted from the coach, permitting herself to be assisted, Joseph's heart shrank to the size of an acorn. Her hand grasped his, squeezed it softly, and there was a kind of caress as their hands parted, like a pale and indistinct breath of wind. In those circumstances, startled by carriages, coaches, barouches, droshkies, or coupés, oblivious to the splashes of mud and the clouds of dust raised by the wheels and the horses' hooves, Herr Strauss at no point felt afraid (and consequently his heart did not shrink to the size of a flea), but neither did he display an impetuous nature (and for that reason his heart did not swell to the size of a quince). He merely discovered the taste of care, the new, unfamiliar care that small hands and slender wrists, as fragile as glass, should not shatter. And, happily, they did not.

Firstly, he had found a small, elongated, bluish envelope, without a seal, name, or address. The envelope had been slipped under the door to his surgery and lay waiting for him on the parquet, by the doormat. He examined it closely, stroking it, turning it over, holding it up to the light, passing it beneath his nostrils. If it had a vague scent, it was more a brackish whiff of glue than any perfume. The dentist opened it using the first scalpel he laid hands on, one with a short, gleaming blade. The paper in the envelope, white, folded in four, was inscribed in violet ink on one side with a short, unsigned sentence. It was a curt, elliptical message, as between conspirators: *Holy Apostles, on the feast day.* After some moments of bewilderment, tallied by the clock on the wall as one and three-quarter minutes, Joseph all of a sudden let out a deep breath; he leaned against the cold stove and glimpsed in the blade of the scalpel not only snatches of his own smile, but also a pair of blue and haughty eyes. Throughout the rest of the day, as he tended to ailing teeth, he caught himself whistling a number of times. Oddly, into his mind and onto his lips returned a childhood ditty he had never liked but that had been dear to his sister Irma and her girlfriends. At one point, the spatula in his hand refused to grip like tweezers. He looked at it askance and laughed. And on the feast of Saints Peter and Paul the Apostles, in the morning, when according to local lore the cuckoo falls silent, when according to the course of the stars the sun had risen for the eighth time since the solstice, and when according to the Wallachian calendar but five days had elapsed since Saint John's Eve and more than two weeks since Whitsun, Joseph Strauss went out into the street early, hoping to rid himself of the hollow feeling in the pit of his stomach. All the color had drained from his freshly shaved cheeks into his cherry-red *lavallière*. He quickly traversed Lipscani Street, the section of Podul Mogoşoaiei this side of the river, and two short lanes on the other side, he skirted the mules of a water seller and some flocks of ducks, he managed to escape from a swarm of tattered urchins by handing out sweets, he passed the ranks of beggars, the expensive carriages drawn up in the shade, and the prattling coachmen, he glimpsed the spires and belfry of Holy Apostles, then the church in its entirety, and pale as he was, paler than ever, he entered. It took him some time to accustom himself to the gray air within, because even the hundreds of candles lit on the feast of the church's patron saints were no match for the glaring sun outside. Later, when the air was no longer gray but had acquired yellowish and ruddy glints, in the midst of the liturgy and many genuflections, under the flowing voices of the priests and the ardent exhalations of the choir, Joseph espied a beige shawl in the apse to the left of the altar. That shawl, which covered the hair, nape, and back of a woman, had once sheltered a little boy and girl shivering in a mad June downpour. Trying to make out the distant figure, he remembered his intensifying twinges of joy since those seconds when Elena Duković, in the sprung carriage that bore them over the Outer Market Bridge, had whispered that she was not the children's mother, but a kind of nanny. The hollowness in the pit of his stomach now vanished, and other twinges, perhaps imaginary, crinkled the folds of his shirt. He emerged toward noon, one of the first worshippers to leave, and waited on a hummock of earth across the road. In the pale blue air he saw as though in the palm of his hand the lines, ornaments, and porch of that church, which, although not Serbian, was now in the custodianship of that nation. And through the broad doorway streamed variegated ranks of people wearing clean, festive attire, in whose tailoring and cloth could be read the weight of each purse. Toward the end of the crowd there appeared a green, billowing dress, like a miracle that had come to pass. They gazed at each other: he did not notice the lace collar, the amber necklace, or the shoes the color of rich butter; she did not discern the gold pin of the *lavallière* or the spherical buttons of the waistcoat. They went over to the poplar tree near the steps, where candles for the living were burning. They lit their candles, brushing each other's hand as if by chance. Thanks to that touch, Joseph Strauss departed with a new note, which he gripped tightly, while Elena Duković departed with a rose in her hand, a rosebud from his buttonhole. As she moved into the distance, she sometimes pressed the flower to her chest.

On the hill above Saint Venera, he hired a carriage at the Hereasca rank, where dozens of horse-drawn cabs gathered, and ordered the driver to take him to Hereşti. The journey was long and sweltering, proceeding first by way of the Beilicul Bridge to the south, then veering west between hovels and vegetable patches, losing itself once more in a southerly direction, amid pastures and stubble fields from which the corn had but lately been reaped, and finally heading west yet again, following the large flocks of crows flying in the same direction. The manor house, without a veranda, arches, or carved posts, had nothing in common with the boyar manses of the plain. From afar, as much as the scattered orchards allowed, Joseph could make out a grayish-white, rigorously geometrical shape upon which a bronze crust was now forming as the sun emerged from the clouds. He realized that he would not arrive late at the manor, that he had managed to keep his promise to the charming couple of princely rank, he neither short nor tall, solidly built and droll, with bristling mustaches, she tiny and pale, with a slightly querulous voice and an inquisitive mien. Out of habit, he grasped the handle of his calfskin bag, from which he had once scraped the initial S, and placed it in his lap. He examined the instruments, powders, and liquors therein, and flicked a fly off the brim of his hat resting beside him on the banquette. In his pocket was the note he had received on the feast of Saints Peter and Paul the Apostles. He extracted it with care and read it once again. He knew its contents by heart, as short and as opaque as those of the first missive, and he no longer sought the logic of the words, but rather the little truths hidden in the tracing of the letters, the way in which Elena Duković had held the pen and guided the nib over the paper. The horses at last ceased to trot and advanced at a walk up a graveled drive. And Joseph no longer delved into illusions and chimeras, but saw in succession an imposing church, an arched gateway, beneath which he passed, clumps of marigolds and cress at the edges of the road, a greyhound bounding idly alongside the horses, patches of azure sky between the plum-white clouds, an ash tree with a huge crown, long rows of vines descending a sandy hillside, the somnolent river in the valley. Elena Duković was sitting on the freshly mown grass with the children, her eyes fixed upon him, behind the gentleman with the bushy mustaches and the lady with the bluish-white cheeks. His hosts greeted him with courtesy and warmth, and the little boy and girl, blending whim with breeding (and bashfulness), decided to bow awkwardly and tell him in clumsy Romanian that they were delighted to see him again. As he was preparing to kiss Elena's hand, having uttered sufficient pleasantries to the masters of the place about the journey, the landscape, and the scorching heat in Bucharest, the greyhound took upon itself to sniff his boots and to jump up with its muzzle between his legs. Herr Strauss almost lost his balance, hesitated, and then, holding the dog by the nape of its neck, brushed his lips over Elena Duković's cool, delicate skin. They all laughed, and talking of lemonade and coffee—and of teeth only in passing—they continued that theatrical performance consummately contrived by Elena Duković. Somewhere in the shade, without any inkling of the roles in which they had been cast (after Baron Nikolić of Rudna had called at Joseph Strauss's surgery on Lipscani Street on the exact day and at the precise hour announced in the note, to thank him for how gallantly he had behaved during the downpour at the Whitsun Fair and to invite him to his estate), they lit cigars on the hill above the plum tree orchard, they sampled a drop of cognac, and drank white wine (the men), they kept their ankles pressed together and the hems of their dresses below their knees, fluttering fans and eyelashes, and drank sherbet (the women), they munched walnuts, leafed through atlases, and poked each other under the table with blunt sticks (the children). Romanian, though spoken hesitantly and ungrammatically by both, proved to be their only common language, and the hosts abandoned it only rarely, when they addressed the servants and the dog, all of whom understood only Serbian. A dry breeze was blowing, presaging the noonday heat, and so they rose reluctantly and headed toward the oak doors that were waiting ajar. At the height of summer and, more especially, sensing the footsteps of Elena Duković on the flagstones, Joseph felt well in that spacious, cool house. He was conducted into a brightly lit room, where an armchair, clean towels, and a small table with arabesque inlays, on which to deploy his medical arsenal, awaited him. In the sunlit corner of the window, on that third day of July 1868, he examined in turn molars, premolars, wisdom teeth, and milk teeth, recording everything meticulously in a notebook, but from a certain point onward he refused to write any more, because he wished with all his soul to commit it to memory. Alone in the room, in the final scene of the performance, Miss Duković and he embraced, and in embracing they made it understood that their embrace might be endless. Or at least very long in duration.

For a while, the fates proved generous to Joseph Strauss. And adroit. At lunch after his consultation with his five patients, while he was absorbed in a piping-hot plate of cockerel borscht, they gave him the idea and, undoubtedly, they inspired in him the courage, to declare that the nanny's gums were ailing. He was met with an astonished look from the head of the table, where the master of the manor was biting into a chicken leg dotted with specks of fat. And from the adjacent chair, the mistress of the house, who was chewing a lovage leaf, stared at him sidelong. He did not hasten to enter into details, first tasting a chili pepper and then rapidly drinking a few spoonfuls of soup to douse the hot coals on his tongue. After he had blown his nose and his eyes had stopped streaming, he explained that the gleaming white of Miss Duković's teeth was mere deceptive appearance. He frightened them with strange words—extraction, alveolar pyorrhea, pathology, and so on and so forth—describing a hidden malady, which in both German and French was called *parodontose*. And that malady, of which Herr Strauss spoke learnedly and measuredly, induced dreadful pain. He drank some wine, examined the newly arrived platters, one with mushrooms stewed in cream, another with browned leg of roast pork, sprinkled with marjoram, paprika, and slices of beetroot, he sighed pensively, and said that for the young nanny a serious plan of treatment was required. He recommended two sessions a week for at least three months. He left the piece of roast meat on his plate to repose in its steam and sauce while he employed copious medical terms, giving a diagnosis for each member of the Nikolić family, four bland verdicts, incapable of causing concern. They dedicated themselves to the chewing of tender meat and mellow mushrooms. A servant vanished behind a door, and from outside the supple and impertinent greyhound was heard to bark. Over dessert, as the flies buzzed gently and languor settled over the walnut table, they agreed that the dentist should pay them another visit that Friday. On Monday, for it was a Monday and according to Joseph's calculations there were another ninety hours until Friday, the nanny and the children withdrew for their afternoon nap. The children bid him farewell as if reciting part of a beginner's lesson in good manners. The others proceeded to take their coffee, to converse and yawn, until that gentleman who was neither short nor tall, with a tendril of cream clinging to his bushy mustaches, asked, at his guest's request, that the carriage be drawn up to the steps. And the fates were not idle. They kept tally of the hours without losing count. They kept watch over Herr Strauss, and saw to it that he slept at least part of the night, that he did not neglect to feed his tomcat, or squander his reserves of schnapps, that he made the journey over the Wallachian plain once more, that he tended to a canine tooth belonging to the lady with the pale cheeks, polished the yellowed incisors of the baron, and helped the little boy rid himself of his first milk tooth, that he took Elena Ducović in his arms once more, in the silence of that luminous room, and finally he rubbed the tip of her tongue with a thick camphorated paste, so that from her breath it would seem that the treatment had begun. There, at Hereşti, where the sun was still searing and the starlings more numerous than the crows, the fates decided that their protégé should listen and be mindful. He heard the drawling voice of Theodor Nikolić of Rudna describing the house, while they sampled a cloudy, cooling liquid that might equally have been called raki, ouzo, or mastika. The polished, grayish-white stone had arrived two hundred and thirty years before from the quarries at Rusçuk, and the manor house, highly symmetrical and full of right angles, with an upper floor, two entrances to the vaulted cellars, a pantiled roof, eight identical arched windows facing the plain, and six windows on the side facing the garden, had been constructed by Hungarian masons entirely according to the tastes and plans of two brothers, the Năsturel boyars, the oldest having had an old and strange name, Cazan, ("cauldron"), and the younger, a lover of calligraphy and printing presses, enjoyed the same rare quality as the liqueur they now savored, for he was known by three different names, in his case Oreste, Iorest, and Udriște. The aroma of aniseed invigorated them and allowed them to imagine that the heat of that summer was pleasantly bearable, and so it was that they went on to explore the history of the house's large belvedere, with its two stories and redbrick walls, plastered to imitate stone, and built some three decades previously at the behest of the penultimate master of the domain. And that master, around whom swirled a host of tangled tales, exploits cruel or magnanimous, illustrious or shameful, lucrative, cunning, amorous, worthy, villainous, and astonishing, deeds dedicated in turn to his nation, to himself, to the Ottomans, to the Wallachians, to the Father, to the Son, to the Immaculate Virgin, and to the Holy Ghost, had been none other than Miloš I, *knjaz* of Serbia for quarter of a century, forced to abdicate in 1839 and recalled to the throne nineteen years later, upon which, having meanwhile grown old, he rested and fretted until his ascension to the heavens in 1860. All these things were now recounted by his nephew, Theodor, as he sprawled on the soft cushions of a wicker armchair, running the fingers of his left hand through his mustaches and occasionally lifting, with his right, the mouthpiece of a hookah to his lips. He inhaled deeply and without haste exhaled thick clouds of smoke, through which the boundless expanses, the plains, the valley, the glittering water of the Argeş, and the scattered trees could no longer be glimpsed. Joseph preferred to puff on his pipe and sit cross-legged. And as he sat, puffing and idling, he learned that Miloš Obrenović had purchased the domain and the manor house from a descendent of the Năsturel boyars, Constantine, a general floundering in debt, that he had built the new outbuildings and stables and renovated the church (of the Holy Trinity), reinforcing the corbels, closing off the porch, and demolishing the wall between narthex and nave, that he had paid for two massive bronze bells to be cast and brought from Budapest, that he had bitten his lips until they bled when his oldest son, Milan III, had been killed just three weeks before his enthronement, that he had sighed heavily when his other son, Mihailo I, lost the crown to the family's deadly foe, Prince Alexander Karadjordjević, that he had knelt and sobbed, his shoulders slowly quaking, on the passing of his older brother Milan I to the world of the righteous, he too an erstwhile *knjaz*, whose red marble tomb could be found there, by the very church at which they, the dentist and the baron, were now looking. At this, they fell silent and waited for their glasses to be refilled. The silence was broken by the footfalls of a servant and on the graveled terrace in the shade they once again watched as the liqueur clouded like whey when mixed with cold water fresh from the well. They drank without clinking glasses, and Herr Strauss observed that the other liquid, in the glass bowl of the hookah, had also changed color, reddening as the tobacco smoke bubbled through it.

At last, the baron gave a vague frown; annoyed at his own thoughts, he scornfully muttered something about women, and moved on to a description of an aunt by marriage, Margiolitza or Maria, née Catargi, now Obrenović, a widow who had stolen the wits and the vigor of Cuza not long ago and was now living in exile alongside the former Romanian sovereign, while her son, a lad of fourteen, had just been proclaimed Prince of Serbia. Although the dentist was by no means one for palace intrigues or alcove whispers, he pricked up his ears and shifted in his seat, startled by this revelation. He even gave a light cough, hoping that the subject would not be abandoned. And it was not. The gentleman who was neither short nor tall, who, it goes without saying, had himself aspired to the throne of his native land, was planning to go to Belgrade for a month, perhaps for the rest of the summer, because the gates of the city had reopened a few days before when the young Milan IV had returned the family blazon to its rightful place. Joseph wished to ask whether Elena Duković would accompany the little girl and boy over the Danube, but as he did not dare, he asked the baron where all those rusty anchors that looked like the claws of a dragon had come from. His host blinked, swallowed the liqueur he was rolling around in his mouth, and turned to look at the three pieces of iron, arranged around a robinia in the courtyard. They were from the ships of Miloš Obrenović, from the years when he had acquired a monopoly on salt, in the reign of Vodă Ghika, and his fleet tirelessly sailed down the river in the valley. On his departure, the dentist, still in the hands of the fates, heard through one of the windows, perhaps from the children's bedroom, the low voice of the nanny. She was humming a Serbian lullaby, to which he for one could have listened until nightfall. But the baron was extending his hand to bid him farewell.

And not only did she have small and slender wrists, she had feet and ankles to match. Examining her boots, Joseph marveled at their unnatural smallness; they looked like doll's footwear. What remained mysterious to him above all was how Elena Duković managed to keep her balance and how she managed to tread so smoothly, as if floating. Her steps, whether she walked at leisure or in a hurry, resembled in his imagination the flight of a bird. And that gliding, as insecure as any flight, demanded to be guarded, like her small hands and slender wrists, as fragile and brittle as glass. In their frequent walks, inhaling her perfume, gazing upon her profile, feeling her discreet touches, he refrained from many things and was careful, very careful, that this woman in the unusual situation of taking treatment for a nonexistent malady should not stumble against the many rocks on the streets of Bucuresci, that she should not slip in the mud of the gutters, that she should not be bitten by the dogs or twist her ankle on any curb, stair, or pothole. The good Lord saw to it that she did not twist her ankle.

To them the summer seemed short and not at all sultry, even though the relentless heat melted men and withered hapless animals alive. The fury of the sun paled before the ardor of their hearts: they perspired, they grew faint, their faces were flushed, but they ascribed their frissons and fevers to the fire of love. After her employers had set off for Belgrade, drawn like moths to the flickering crown, Elena had left the estate at Hereşti and settled into a poky room off the courtyard of the palace owned by grandees of the Nikolić family of Rudna, in the Udricani quarter of Bucharest, where the rumbling of the carriages, the whinnying of the horses, and the cries of the millet-beer hawkers were incessant. The way from there to the surgery of the German doctor who was endeavoring to heal her gums was not long, and so, twice a week, with the baron's permission, she would inform the baron's overseer that she was going out for a few hours, on foot, in order to be treated for her ailment. In that room with its waxed floors and Anatolian carpet, with its chair by the window, a chair with a single, central leg and a reclining back (upholstered in navy blue velvet), next to the display cabinet with its host of potions, powders, and surgical instruments, next to the anatomical charts hanging on the walls, they sought and slowly discovered each other, but not completely, for they both knew (or at least had an inkling of) the meaning of propriety and esteem. During so many conversations, in the pauses between words, silences, and illusions, the skirts of Miss Duković were never lifted all the way, each visit they ascended a further one or two inches, in the latter part of July they had reached a little above the knee, then, at the beginning of August, halfway up the thigh, and finally, when the calendars were preparing to usher in the month of September, a mere palm's width higher, sufficient for the quivering, milky white skin—velvety as not even velvet can be—to be caressed. And it was caressed, at leisure, lightly, with the tips of the fingers, with the fingers entire, with the forehead, with the nose, with the chin. Sometimes, suspended in the fluid of time, while the tweezers, chisels, needles, spatulas, pipettes, and forceps coyly kept watch, their mouths seemed inseparable, and their tongues writhed together, coiling and ravenous. One Wednesday, just as the noise of Lipscani was coming to a boil, it happened that the hem of her skirt remained in its proper place at her ankles, and instead it was her bodice, fastened with small green buttons, that yielded. Thin and pale, with his chestnut hair and hazel eyes, with his inscrutable (fortunate and sorrowful, Berlinese and Balkanic, joyful and agonizing) histories, Joseph Strauss buried his face in the breast of Elena Duković and wept. He was not pushed away, neither when he unfastened the sixteen buttons nor when he let the cloth and the lace glide down naked shoulders, nor when he suddenly laughed, as though in his soul there were not enough room for all the things that had accumulated therein. His tears moistened her breasts, they mingled with droplets of perspiration and trickled down to her belly, they ran around her navel and flowed ever lower, and Elena clasped his neck in her arms and squeezed him tightly, as tightly as she could, until they lost count of the moments and one of her nipples, who knows which, found its way between his lips. And that nipple, like a ripe bramble, somehow bulged and, in time, began to throb and to breathe like a swallow's chick. Thinking of soaring and of flight, Joseph removed one of her sandals, the right, kissed the pink foot and nibbled the big toe, which quivered and tried to touch the firmament of his palate. The young woman slipped her hands under her dress, seeking to disencumber herself of her garters, of her white linen undergarments, her slip, her silk stockings, all that was underneath. Herr Strauss, the dentist, even if he did not at that moment regard himself as a German or a doctor, clasped her hands and prevented her. Without his head intruding beneath the pleats of her dress, but rather from above, he kissed the small hollow between her thighs, firmly, where the hair must have been as black as her tresses, curlier and sparser. Then he lifted her from the blue velvet of the upholstered chair, and while Elena kept her eyes shut and her teeth clenched, he bore her in his arms, making a circuit of the room, rocking her and whispering to her a host of things, as though to a child with a fever.

Although they had never ascended to the first floor of his redbrick house, Joseph decided one morning, while draining a cup of tea, that it was, at last, time for his two loves to meet. And so he carried downstairs the wicker basket, very early, before any bleary-eyed tradesmen could knock at the door of his surgery, their jaws swollen and teeth doused in alcohol. Entering after lunch, Miss Duković, who was wearing a beige hat and had just folded her parasol, came across a sleeping tomcat with one white ear, one black, lolling on the dentist's chair. It was as though he, too, were waiting to be rid of aching gums. The tomcat's eyes blinked open, and, moving only the tip of his tail, he regarded her at length, as if she were a fairy from his feline dreams.

In all their walks through blazing Bucharest, they never ceased telling each other the stories of their lives. Since the overseer of the houses of Theodore Nikolić of Rudna was negligent as to the comings and goings of the nanny, being more concerned with carafes of red wine, with keeping the woodpile full, with sleeping, with repairing the drainpipes and window shutters, with the haunches of the kitchen women, with the grooming of the stallions in the stables, and with how the dice fell when he played backgammon or shot craps for handsome sums, Elena often found reasons to go out, concocting more lies in these weeks than she had uttered in the past ten years put together. Totting up her fabrications, one afternoon Herr Strauss deduced her age, for he had never ventured to ask her. At the age of thirty-two (and a half), he felt old, but that thought quickly evaporated. Their meetings took place in secret, at none too customary hours, and they had to find deserted, hidden-away areas of the city, where they would not bump into any acquaintances of the baron or his servants. At least at first, in July, Joseph racked his brains in search of spots where they might meet each other or winding lanes along which they might walk. And so it was that for three whole weeks Miss Duković adored the brioche and poppy-seed cakes of Peter Bykow, crossing the threshold of his shop almost daily after lunch, when the canicular heat was at its height. She would buy two of each, and with the parcel in her hands, always looking at the floorboards and not the baker's face, she would enter the back room through an annoyingly squeaky door. There, where everything was white with flour dust, sitting on a clean checked blanket laid over a heap of sacks, she would await the dentist, the healer of her heart, if not her gums. She did not permit herself to remain within for more than a quarter of an hour, but in that brief segment of time, as tart as a slice of strudel, they would grow dizzy. It was also then, around the middle of the month, that they profited from the feast of Saint Elijah and took shelter in the courtyard of the Stavropoleos Church Inn, sitting on some peeled logs, and she stuffed his head with the virtues, travails, and good deeds of the prophet, also describing to him a few Serbian customs, especially those linked to plum brandy and beekeeping. As women had no business at a barber's, they were unable to enjoy the immediate help of Otto Huer, but they received the gift of his most cunning ideas. The barber, compassionate toward the amours of moggies and dear human friends alike, remembered that he knew Vasile, the warden of Colței Tower, an eternally jolly fat man with nine children. And so, thanks to his lather brush, razor, and scissors, to his prattle during the moments when the cheeks of the warden were thickening with foam and the bristles were vanishing between the thin, narrow blade, the two lovers were able to climb to the top of the tallest structure in the city. They were not interested in spotting far-off fires and they did not think of the tower's builders (Swedish soldiers from the army of Karl XII, roaming the East after the defeat at Poltava). They counted the steps, one hundred and eighty-eight, they had no idea that there had been two hundred and fourteen (until the devastating earthquake of October 1802, which had lopped off the building's peak), they gazed into the distance, astonished and embracing, silent, perspiring for all too many reasons: the stifling heat, the spiral ascent, the joy, the insatiability, and also affection for the hundreds of swallows that had made their nests beneath the eaves. From high above, Bucharest revealed itself as they could never have imagined it. The clouds of dust that followed the carts and carriages looked like minuscule flecks, the roofs and chimneys awaited the rain and the cold, the spires of the churches and the belfries no longer scraped the sky, the waters of the Dîmbovitza gleamed brightly and those of the Bucureştioara dully, the palace of the prince, from which Carol I was absent (driven away by the sweltering heat, by affairs of state, and by boredom), was no more majestic than the boyar houses, the vacant lots looked brownish red and the clusters of woodland a dusty green, the color of olives immersed in brine, the hospital, the school, and the monastery at the base of the tower seemed stunted, one hundred and fifty thousand souls were at their feet, each living by his own law and all by the laws of the prince and the United Principalities, eating or dozing (because it was that time of day), breathing and sweating. Joseph, who knew that he was not in midair but for all that believed that he was flying, withdrew his hand from hers and sought something in the pocket of his waistcoat. He pulled out a gilded watch on a chain, and on the back of its lid two names were engraved, *Gertrude* and *Irma*. And, in accordance with their good habit of telling the stories of their lives, not in chronological order but all in a jumble, he began to describe to Miss Duković something he had described to no other: how his mother and sister had perished, consumed in a fire. First he told her about a poisonous mushroom, *Amanita muscaria*, red with white pimples, which the people beneath their eyes, in the city stretched below, called snake's hat or snake mushroom, and some called *Fliegenpilz*, about how it could be dried and powdered, about the enchanted powers of the tea prepared from the fine dust, somewhat like the gifts of opium, but more seductive and restful, about the longing that those who tasted the brew would have to drink it once more, about their desire no longer to know about anything or anyone, about their flight from the world, about the serenity and acceptance that could be read on their faces, about their vast indifference. Absorbed by this treacherous tea, which he himself, a young lad fascinated by the glass vials and miracles of the laboratory, had on a number of occasions prepared for them, his mother and sister had slowly grown distant from their fellow men, they had set out along the road of stars and beatitude, one evening of blustering wind they had forgotten about the kettle on the hob, leaving it to buckle and burst into flame, afterward (perhaps) applauding the flames, (perhaps) blowing on them, allowing them to overwhelm the curtains, carpets, furniture, thick-beamed walls, and (perhaps) even their bodies. He felt a dreadful pain in his chest, it was suffocating him, but he managed to swallow some of the scorching afternoon air when Elena did not try to discover the recipe for the tea, but simply embraced him, tightly. Somewhere toward the horizon, hazy outlines could be made out, and the dentist leaned his elbows on the balustrade under the shingle roof. He examined them for a long time, then gave a start, on realizing that they were the Carpathians.

Slowly he and Elena descended the rickety, winding steps, careful not to scrape the ceiling with the crowns of their heads or bump against the doorjambs. Below, in the arched passageway of the tower, where not only ordinary folk but even circus stilt-walkers would have had ample headroom, they straightened their backs and smiled. Joseph was thinking of the fat Vasile, always huffing and puffing up the minaret-like stair, and Elena Duković was not thinking of anything, she merely felt like smiling. Soon enough, however, they remembered the insufferable face of the overseer, their sole enemy. At a quarter past three, Dušan, the Nikolić family's trusty man, would certainly be snoring in a cellar of the Udricani quarter, taking his siesta on a straw mattress, but his eyes saw through those of others and his ears heard many things. As ever, Herr Strauss set off first, the nanny following him twenty paces behind, so that it would never occur to anyone that they were walking together or that there was any connection between them. They headed downhill, toward the Catholic church, leaving behind them the Kiesch Hotel, the old Austrian consulate, the courtyard of Doctor Marsille, and the freshly whitewashed façade of the Hagi-Moscu Palace. Before them lay a long lane and the future, gentle and overrun with the flurry of drying sheets, as the dentist hoped, mysterious and resounding with the prattle of children, as Miss Duković imagined, but first they would have to traverse the weeks at the tail end of summer and, before that, bring to a close the days that abode under the zodiacal sign of fire. They did not hurry. They felt good, warm, they found no reason to rush. In the shops of the Colței Inn, while Joseph was admiring the saddles, harnesses, bridles, and spurs in a window, a woman with tiny boots, like a doll's, passed alongside him, lightly touched his shoulder, then swung her parasol and went on her way in her blue dress, as though she were floating. When she had gone some twenty paces, the doctor abandoned looking at the items of harness laid out on shelves and hanging from hooks, and strolled on. Halfway across the fenced-in vacant lot next to the Kalinderu Church, over the road from the Bucuresciu Caravanserai (where the windows were covered by thick white drapes, behind which the Sultan's emissaries were dozing or cooling themselves with infusions of mint, lemon, and aniseed), Elena stopped for a while, opened her parasol with a snap, and adjusted the brim of her hat, allowing the tall thin man who had been standing stock-still on the pavement to overtake her by almost twenty paces. Thus they walked, until the macadam disappeared and the lane was paved with wooden beams. Then they grew smaller and smaller and veered left, one after the other, vanishing from the gaze of a fat man with nine children, who, watching them from the pinnacle of the highest structure in the city, was chortling and hiccoughing.

In time, their precautions and fear began to wither away, and a reckless kind of courage sprouted in them like a vigorous plant, an invisible, climbing ivy that quickly overran them. Without having suggested or even discussed it, they tacitly abandoned their perambulations through outlying areas, through forsaken quarters and churchyards, and still roaming here and there, they shortened the distance between them by twenty paces, or left it to its fate, as if they had retreated from barren territories like soldiers losing their patience, rhythm, and purpose. Ever further from the flocks of ducks, geese, guinea fowl, hens, and turkeys, ever more rarely having to skirt the dead bodies of horses, donkeys, pigs, dogs, oxen, and goats, ever more guarded against the stench of slops and mounds of garbage (for, as far as smells went, Bucharest had its nuances), glimpsing ever more rarely the banks of the Dîmbovitza, crowded with lopsided houses, washerwomen, watermills, pigsties, and rats, the dentist and the nanny drew nearer to the belly of that huge body. And the city pulsed peacefully. Like two points on its imaginary map, Joseph Strauss and Elena Duković moved in decreasing concentric circles toward where the cityscape and the air grew cleaner. They walked side by side and separately, as was their wont, proceeding along Podul Mogoşoaiei, conquering the street yard by yard, day by day, convinced that the throne was the absolute center of the city, because the sovereign, in the late August heat, might be anywhere, whereas the princely throne, massy and heavy, remained in place. One Wednesday, they ventured from the Zlătari Inn, at the end of Lipscani Street, all the way to the crossroads, where they could glimpse the handsome Bărcănescu house. Joseph could not rid himself of a nagging cough, which was not the result of a cold but of nervousness, and Miss Duković, following behind him, slightly frowning, hesitant, preoccupied with that nasty cough, heedless of the crows that flew slantwise against the clouds. On Thursday they did not choose the Sărindar and Hotel Oteteleşeanu side of the street, but the other side, and they went as far as the Pasha Kapuşi gate, by the old palace from the reign of Caragea Vodă. Had someone sprung from the earth or bare stone (for this street alone was paved) and wondered what the one was doing following the other, why they kept pausing and touching in passing, why they were smiling and casting glances at each other, Herr Strauss would have been ready with the answer that they had set out in search of a medicament for inflamed gums at the Brus Pharmacy, the Slătineanu store, or the La Fortuna Pharmacy, where Adolf Steege sold his remedies. On Friday, he acting the part of the doctor and she the patient, they passed by the library in the building of the former municipal courts, by the Gothic façade of the Small Theatre, by the wine emporium of C. A. Rosetti, by a hairdressing salon (Miss Duković, under her hat, was wearing her hair fastened with four pins), and by the inn of Friedrich Bossel, an Austrian, proprietor of the Romanian Arcade (paved with flagstones, roofed with yellow glass, and swarming with merchants). On their way back, at a brief, barely perceptible signal from the dentist, they entered the studio of Szathmari. Inside, where everything was reminiscent of an alchemist's laboratory, the complicated birthing of photographs and lithographs abated, temporarily entrusted to the apprentices, and the master hastened to greet his guests, giving instructions for Turkish coffee to be prepared. They drank from small cups, blowing on the hot liquid, crushing the coarse froth with their teaspoons, and fidgeting on the soft chairs. Apart from the news and commentaries in the papers, Joseph had learned nothing about Karl Ludwig except that he took delight in watercolors by Preziosi, a painter who had recently arrived from Istanbul. This last detail, and the memories it stirred, stung him like salt sprinkled in a wound. He did not sigh, but after a few more pleasantries, they rose to take their leave. After each had passed Sunday in his and her own church, Joseph in the cool of the Catholic cathedral, attending the Roman mass, digesting events on an empty stomach, praying, occasionally twitching, Elena at the Saint Nicholas Udricani church in her own neighborhood, inhaling the incense-laden, Orthodox air, making hundreds of signs of the cross, daydreaming, they met again on Monday and resumed their advance up Podul Mogoșoaiei, passing the Hugues Hotel, the Grand Theatre, the piano emporium of Jakob Rink, the adjacent Romanian Club, with the invisible but ever present mist exuded by its English Masonic rituals, the Lazarus and Coriolano stores, and the stores across the road in the Kretzulescu Inn. In front of a shop sign inscribed *Giovanni Confiseur* they gazed into each other's eyes, they restrained their longing, and each thought with compassion of the other and with joy of him- and herself, because Herr Strauss was expecting at home a block of nougat and almond cookies, gifts from Martin Stolz, the notary's assistant, and Elena Duković had learned that morning that she was to be welcomed home with plum dumplings and walnut syrup cake, prepared by the cook of the Nikolić of Rudna family. And on Wednesday, having tucked all thoughts of sweetmeats somewhere deeply away, they at last reached the royal palace, viewing it in detail first from the wing by the guardhouse, then from an acute angle in the Bishopric Gardens. The dentist knew all too well where the throne room lay, and so he was more interested in the profile of Miss Duković, while she, gazing at the opaque windows, was left with the mystery unsolved. To passers-by and cabmen idling at the corner, the two both did and did not seem strangers. It was not until a Saturday, September 2, that they cleared up this confusion, when they stood in front of a shop window clasping each other's hands and pressing their shoulders together, laughing softly and imagining what it would be like at their wedding if Joseph Strauss were to wear that cylindrical and dreadfully tall hat invented by M. Jobin, the French proprietor of the store. They left arm in arm, still laughing, and then suddenly they fell silent, realizing that this was the first time they had talked of marriage. After that, they did not head toward Giovanni Confiseur but to the Fialkowsky cake shop by the Grand Theatre, in the Torok building. They were sitting in a sunlit spot by the window, cutting their cake with their spoons and munching at leisure, when through the door came Dušan, in his best clothes, and sat down without greeting them. He placed his elbows on the table and rested his chin on his palms. Scowling.

6 ✤ Hubbub and Babies

CLIMBING FILARET HILL in a gently rattling coach, with the horses bridled at a walk, Elena was wearing a voluminous dress, but not so voluminous yet that she could not go out in public. On the next to last day of October, when the fading year 1869 unleashed its winds, her desire to see the railroad, to hear the whistle of the locomotive, and to travel down to the Danube, was great, infinitely greater than her bulging belly, which according to the hunches and calculations, had been growing for about five months. She was shielded from the cold by a lined cloak, a velvet bonnet, the beige shawl from which she was so rarely parted, and the right arm of the dentist, which clasped her around the shoulders. Before the conveyance conquered the slope, however, and before the outline of the station loomed over the rows of vines, in fact before they even climbed into the coach, before her belly began to swell, and before she began to have bouts of morning sickness, she had ceased to be called Duković. It had happened the previous autumn, pages now torn from the calendars, soon after she had tasted that cake with whipped cream and marzipan. She had seen first of all the handle of a dagger in the waistband of the estate overseer, the blade had gleamed in the Fialkowsky cake shop under the table, and the lips of the overseer, as if spitting, had cast dreadful words in Serbian and Romanian meant to terrify them both, Joseph had attempted to riposte, but the point of the knife had pressed him ever more heavily below the liver. The overseer had led her to the door, gripping her elbow tight as a vice, he thrust her into a gig, and tied her hands behind her back, he did not swear, he did not curse, he merely scowled and goaded the chestnut stallion into a gallop. When they arrived at the house in Udricani he shut Elena up in her room and padlocked the door. On the sixth night of her imprisonment she was kidnapped by a hired thief with a concealed face and a reconciled soul, one who was fond of garlic, to be exact. And that thief had made the sign of the cross on the preceding night, the fifth, when he had for the first time softly unfastened the padlock and the lady had refused to dress and flee, but instead calmly sat down to write in the pitch blackness, taking care not to dip the nib too deeply into the inkpot, and handed him an envelope for the gentleman who had engaged his services. The envelope, as Herr Strauss was to discover half an hour later, was blue and elongated, without seal, insignia, name, or address, and vaguely redolent of brackish glue. In the letter Elena Duković asked him to swear with his hand on the Bible and then with his hand on the pen, consigning his oath to paper, that they would be married in an Orthodox church, that their numerous children would be baptized in the same place, that he would not succumb to a mania for strong drink or the vice of philandering, that he would not touch the mushroom tea as long as he lived, neither to drink it himself nor to prepare it for others, that he would not forget to hug her, and that he would never invite her to a Polish cake shop again. And he swore. In German, uttering the words softly, but distinctly enough to make Siegfried prick up his black ear, and then he sat down before a sheet of white paper, with the inkpot and a goose quill at the ready. The wedding, because that modest gathering of seven people and one tomcat was still a wedding, was held on a Wednesday, at ten o'clock in the morning, at the church of Saint Ionică in the Brezoianu quarter. The preparations, such as they were, had been taken care of by their godfather, Calistrache. He had not cooked for the prince in fourteen months, since Karl Ludwig now entrusted his luncheons and dinners to a French chef, but he still lived in a lane behind the royal palace, in a small two-roomed house with whitewashed walls and a shingle roof. And the lanky Calistrache, who had sheltered them there for almost a week, persuaded the parish priest to shrive them, to give them holy communion, and to bind them in holy matrimony at an hour and on a day when it would not have crossed anyone's mind to wed. During the service, while Joseph and Elena wore the wedding crowns, while they processed around the table to the hymn "Dancing Isaiah," while they listened to the rather muffled voice of the priest, while their godmother took the rings out of a cloth and kissed them, while Siegfried sat on a pew lifting the tip of his tail in the air, during all that long and muddled interval in which their dreams were fulfilled, they saw how the perspiring Calistrache strove to stop his shoulder twitching and his eyes blinking. After the ceremony, the party rode in a spacious carriage to the Colentina River, where they laid rugs on the empty riverbank, ate, laughed, and drank, and at four o'clock in the afternoon, when the barber had fallen asleep on the grass, the tomcat had just caught a baby mole, and Joseph's brain was swaying in his head like a pendulum, the groom lifted Elena Strauss in his arms and, fully clothed as she was, instead of carrying her over the threshold of the house at number 18 Lipscani Street he threw her into the shallow water, so that she might be cleansed of evil and her heart be pure.

Filaret Station, as it suddenly loomed in the plain beyond the huge vineyard of the Metropolia, far from the buildings of the city, looked as if it were painted on the sky. Elegant and awkward, unconnected to the world in which it found itself, it endured the harsh wind and the ceaseless assault of souls burning with curiosity, who regarded it as a great marvel. Not even a month after its magnificent inauguration with brass bands, flowers, cannon salvoes, holy water, prayers, wine, and impassioned speeches, including one from prime minister Dimitrie Ghika, affectionately nicknamed by other politicians and the people Beyzade Mitică, the dentist had been swept along by the collective madness and had managed to come by second-class tickets, paying a hefty bribe to someone who had been queuing since the crack of dawn for two reserved seats. With that bit of luck he was able to satisfy the greatest craving of Elena's pregnancy, for she did not dream of baklava, sherbet, caviar, truffles, or pâté de fois gras. Instead, like so many inhabitants of Bucuresci, she wanted to see at close hand the den of the monster ensconced to the south, the long, metallic, puffing serpent that sped faster than cavalry squadrons. She examined the station minutely, first the office building, which was like a synagogue, but lower and broader, then the glass-roofed terminus and the platforms, along which ran rows of lamp posts and small ornamental arches, she gazed upon the perfection of the rails, six parallel lines grouped in three pairs, laid on countless ties, she sneezed softly, so as not to draw glances, and sniffed some camphorated smelling salts. And the serpent, refusing to slither, remained as straight as a ruler and as proud as a cockerel. Then, suddenly awakening into life, it belched smoke, not from nostrils but from a tall, thick chimney, and emerged from its den at precisely the appointed hour, juddering at first as it set in motion, then moving ever more smoothly as it approached its maximum speed, twenty-five miles an hour. The Strausses found themselves in the belly of the iron beast, on a road of iron, fearful lest their gallbladders rebel. They held each other's hands and spoke in whispers, and after a while they forgot to tell each other what they were thinking, falling prey to their own reveries in the swaying train, as the plains unfolded beneath their eyes and the locomotive's whistle gave occasional deafening hoots, when carts, flocks, or people were slow in getting out of the way. In the second-class car, in the middle of that train built in Manchester, at the Aushbury works, Joseph sank into a tangled recollection of the route he had covered from Berlin, in particular its railroad sections. Somewhere by the Călugăreni marshes, he realized that just as he had followed Prince Karl Ludwig three and a half years earlier, as a pale shadow, traversing the same route with a delay of seven weeks, so he was following him now, the only difference being that this time he was accompanied by his young wife (and unborn child), not a tomcat. The major absentee from the inaugural ceremonies of October 19, the sovereign had in fact been the train's first passenger, a privileged one, traveling as far as Giurgiu on the morning of August 26 in the locomotive's cabin, alongside the stoker and the railroad concessionaire, Englishman Trevor Barkley, who had personally bridled the metallic beast, pulling levers and handles. At the end of the summer and at the 42-mile mark, Carol had disembarked and taken an open carriage to the port in Giurgiu, boarded the yacht *Stephen the Great*, and with the wind in his sails he had set off for his native land. Imagining those scenes described in the newspapers, Herr Strauss recalled an episode in his relationship with the former captain of dragoons, their last, lengthy encounter, which had taken place just four evenings before the prince's departure for his homeland. There had been a strange and paradoxical discussion, in which one of them, the prince, though he used harsh words, was excited and overcome with joy by his impending reunion with his family (the first since he had been elevated to the Romanian throne), and the other, the dentist, for all he strove to smile, felt that the bitterness and tension were worsening second by second, bunching up in his chest. They had not seen each other for a long time, and in that interval so many important things had happened that Joseph felt he could no longer take it all in, though he had read reams of newspapers and chatted with friends, patients, and acquaintances (including Siegfried, without learning his opinion).

For example, during a period when the Sublime Porte nursed suspicions that Bucuresci might be assisting groups of Bulgarian insurgents and, at the same time, a rumor was circulating in Western chancelleries that there had arrived in the United Principalities thousands of Germans, all men, ostensibly to work on the railroads but in fact ready to enlist, well, it was precisely then that a law had been passed to restructure the army, an act of the sovereign, government, and parliament, but above all an act of the sovereign, with his barracks past and his military aspirations, an act whereby modern training and recruitment rules were introduced, new regiments were established, new garrisons were planned, corporal punishment and operatic uniforms were abolished, the role of sub-officers was strengthened, and thirty-three militia battalions were formed. Moreover, so that the fundamental intention to reform the army would be clear, Carol had early on appointed to the head of the war ministry a politician, not an officer. Then, further to scatter the mists in the administration, as far as this was possible, he had put an end to the absurd situation whereby the post office and telegraph service were run under the authority of the Austro-Hungarian consulate, a situation which in the past had helped a certain crony of Cuza's — Cezar Librecht, a former sergeant in the Belgian army and deft violator of private correspondence — to get rich by blackmail and the sale of compromising information, even to build himself an astounding house, with neo-Gothic battlements, a Moorish interior, and a wonderful Florentine salon overlooking the garden. On April 1, the elegant palace once built by the logothete Scarlat Bărcănescu on Doamnei Lane was turned into the Central Department of the Post Office and Telegraph Service, a new institution of that fragile and venturesome state, which was striving not to allow other states to poke their noses into its business. Fortunately, and by the grace of God, the harvest of 1868 had been bountiful, so old debts had at last been paid off, functionaries' wages had begun to be paid regularly, and a part of the money had been channeled into the reserve fund, which had been sickly and malnourished, ready at any time to give up the ghost. Although in November the presidency of the council of ministers had passed from the hands of Nicolae Golescu into the palms of Dimitrie Ghika, repeated elections had not given the prince's party a reasonable majority in the Chamber until April of '69, when the opposition had had to content themselves with just ten deputies out of a total of one hundred and fifty. Then, at last, the railroad, another matter which from the very outset had nestled among the sovereign's plans and notes — something capable of dissipating the national torpor and making the jolting mail coaches that linked the land to the rest of the world a thing of the past—seemed to have settled into a groove, although its steps, as in a dance, were sometimes sideways, or two steps forward, one step back. The Offenheim concession, signed and sealed on May 24, '68, had included three northeastern lines, like three deep breaths of air, totaling 140 miles. After a series of parliamentary hesitations and tussles in reaction to Carol's having entrusted the Moldavian concession to a Berlin consortium, led by Dr. Heinrich B. Strousberg, the Dukes of Ratibor and Ujest, and Count Lehndorff, the prince had had the extraordinary pleasure in the autumn of 1868 of signing and promulgating the law for the construction of the railroads, which sealed, among other things, the fate of the Roman–Tecuci–Galatzi line, with its short Tecuci–Bîrlad appendage. It was also around this time, in September, when above Bucuresci there floated not only thousands of crows but also flocks of wild geese (exactly one year before Prince Karl would do the rounds of Weinburg, Brüssel, Baden-Baden, and Paris in search of a bride), that a small festivity had been held in the north of the city, on a former property of Dinicu Golescu, to celebrate the laying of the foundation stone of the Tîrgovişte Station. A long, tall potbellied monster called an omnibus, rolling on wooden wheels and drawn by horses, had begun to run to Filaret. It was no more than a covered wagon, with a door at the back and fourteen seats, with stops at Saint Ştefan, the Stone Bridge, and New Saint George. Folk did not jostle to ride in it, and some spat in their breast when they saw it passing.

Leaning against the wooden backrest of the banquette and careful not to disturb the dozing Elena who was resting her head on his right shoulder, Joseph Strauss continued to gaze through the window of the train, but he both did and did not see the yellowish-gray, red-flecked landscape. His mind was in a great library, where thousands of volumes showed an esteem for the German, French, and Latin languages, where the candles in the candlesticks had just been lit and the aroma of tobacco harmonized with the pattern of the Afghan carpet, and where he learned the secret things that had languished in the deepest recesses of the prince's mind, soul, and even trouser crotch. Coughing more than once, the prince had told him how tangled are the ways of the Lord when bodily desires are aroused, how great the shame can be, at dawn, with testicles drained and soul laid waste, what a miracle it was that the girl was blind, and how good and evil, both together, lay hidden between her thighs, what a pest the mosquitoes were and how agonizing his bout of malaria had been, how much he had hoped that his visit to the Crimea would bring him the hand of a Russian princess in marriage, how devious and slippery Tsar Alexander had proven to be, like a fish, what a silence there was from the continent's royal and imperial families when the question of marriage to a Romanian sovereign came up, how sour the nights were at the age of thirty, and how bitter the evenings, how happy he was to be going to Prussia and how determined he was to come back with a wife, whoever she might be. Pouring the wine and avoiding his eyes, Carol pronounced words such as *gratitude, loyalty, powerlessness, fear, trust, separation, devotion,* and the like. Herr Strauss's fingers gripped the glass with a slight tremor, and his lips did not let it go until it was drained. He must have been very pale, he imagined, as he sat in the second-class railroad car, or perhaps he had blushed, listening, waiting, silent. Karl Ludwig had thanked him assiduously, because he understood like no one else what it meant to be witness to loneliness and distress, to prepare enchanted tea, and, above all, to procure a woman in absolute secrecy for a man who wore a crown. And it was precisely that understanding, as the dentist observed and the prince was torturing himself to say, that was about to sever their relationship like a saber whirling through the heated air of the room, that weighed like a millstone, almost dragging down the ceiling. With convoluted formulations, the prince had confessed to Joseph, who was cold, very cold, how difficult it would be for them to meet again. He asked him to forget what deserved to be forgotten and not to be angry if he never called him to the palace again. He refilled the glasses and begged his forgiveness. They drank. They embraced.

The train slowed as it entered Giurgiu, then made a dreadful screeching noise as it braked. The wind seemed gentler by the Danube, and the river, which they reached in a horse-drawn cab, the same way they had reached Filaret Station, greeted them placidly and dazzlingly, for the sun had managed to break through the clouds. They bought roasted corn, and the old woman who was turning the cobs over the fire, having looked Elena up and down, permitted herself to tell the lady that, given how swollen her belly was, she was sure to give birth to a boy. They all laughed, and Joseph refused the coppers she handed him as change. Then, chatting, husband and wife headed toward a meadow with thistles and hawthorn bushes, beyond the grain silos, barges, and bustle of the port. After a while, once she had finished describing the recipes for some Serbian pies, the kind with meat and vegetables, Elena Strauss went to the riverbank and cupped some water in her palms. She drank. And they embraced.

Like any woman waiting for nine months to elapse, Elena wanted her soul to be at peace. The walls had been white-washed and the floorboards waxed. She had picked out all kinds of cloth and sewn a host of little shirts, diapers, and bonnets. She had knitted sweaters, vests, and socks (so small that they looked like clothes for a tomcat). She had ordered a little green quilt and spent two hours in the workshop making sure that the tradesman stuffed it with clean, new wool, not scraps. She had frequently counted the bundles of wood in the shed in the back yard, and in December (when the price was triple) she had persuaded Joseph to pay for yet another sled of dry logs. She had settled on a light, lindenwood trough in which to bathe the baby and an osier cot in which to put him to bed. She had taken care that the larder lacked for nothing, as a long and tense winter awaited them. She had checked the rushlights and stock of candles. She had scoured the pots with lye and polished the silver cutlery with salt and vinegar. She had asked the wife of Peter Bykow to help her pickle cabbage, cucumbers, and bell peppers (so as not to wrinkle the hands of a pregnant woman). She had slept much and made some changes around the house, guessing that otherwise none of it would be taken care of for quite some time to come. She had called an upholsterer for the chairs in the day room, all of whose backs were ragged and scratched, asking him to replace the velvet with material of the same straw yellow color. She had not understood why Siegfried had turned his back then and crawled under the chest of drawers, with his ears flattened to his head. Just before the pendulum clock struck eleven, while Herr Strauss was still in the ground-floor surgery and she was crooning a song in her native Serbian, the tomcat emerged, lay down on his belly among the balls of wool, and with the pads of his forepaws began to push them softly, very softly, so that the yarn unwound to the rhythm of her knitting needles. Some while ago, placing him in her lap and stroking him, whispering to him, she had persuaded him not to steal her balls of wool, not to roll them around and rip them to shreds. She had not taught him, because he would not have let himself be taught, but from that moment on Siegfried had patiently begun to help her, as if he had known the motion of knitting needles all his life.

In the morning, as the upholsterer made his way through the snow, with his apprentices carting the six chairs behind him, on two of the chair backs it was still possible to read the following:

(cat year fourteen thousand three hundred and eighty-six, month of Fresh Fish, fifth day—April 27, 1869)
Their bodies do not have fur, I tell you, wonderful one, with your flecks like coals, their bodies do not have tails, know you, Manastamirflorinda, with your tufts of flame, they are both as white as yogurt, they are slender, they rustle, they hide beneath coverlets and sheets, behind curtains and doors, the light quivers, the sunbeams stream in tresses and ripples, the candles go wild, the flames dance, shake, flicker, the darkness leaps, day and night merge, fuse, the sheets are cast aside, slide to the floor, and fall dumb, their skin is beaded with dew, I see entwinings, archings, twistings, I hear soft moans, whispers, tender words, perhaps snatches of song, it would not be hard for me to say, vengefully, that humans meow and purr, but you, O queen, you will prick up your ears and you will not blink, your little nostrils, like pomegranate seeds, will snuffle the scent, you will not believe me, I would never lie to you, the sounds of love trickle down the walls and are quenched, my masters tumble onto the rug and are inflamed, her hair is long and black, below her shoulder she has a spot, on her creamy chest have swollen two large round hummocks, like wild mushrooms, are they firm? the hands of the kind doctor touch

them, cup them, tend them, his lips imbibe them, protect them,
there is no need of bandages, scalpel, liquors, he has learned
to heal them, sometimes . . . (here the velvet is torn away,
in the place where the upholsterer had ripped off a scrap
and carefully examined it, pondering the bolts of material
in his shop) . . . *from her movements emanate warm and*
greenish mists, peace settles over the room like a fine powder,
coming through the window, it is not the smoke of the stoves,
it is not the steam from the food on the hob, it is not the
aroma of apples and puddings in the oven, the breeze that
wafts from her gowns is like a caress, I feel it on my nape,
down my spine, under my whiskers, tranquility and joy have
settled over our house, thou, Manastamirflorinda, thou hast
felt the air on thy evening visits, with Otto Huer, the barber
magician, thou hast looked into nooks and chests, among the
books, thou, O queen, hast unfailingly understood that the
heart of my mistress ticks gently, her laughter is as sweet as
milk, I ever strive to find it and drink it, her words are like
partridges, I stalk them and gulp them up, Joseph's eyes seem
drunk, and they have shed all trace of woe.

(the following cat year, the month of Warm Dens, on the
third day—December 4, 1869)
From that huge belly, my love, know thou, fifteen kittens will
emerge, her belly has swollen to the size of a barrel or a sack
of lentils, I am awake before dawn and I wait, I keep watch,
the miracle might happen at any time, from beneath the quilt
there wafts soft breathing, sleep will not be denied, the kittens
lie curled up, they stir and they grow, yet another night
vanishes without them emerging, yet another day arrives on
tiptoes, I divine it, soon the coffee will be boiling in the pot,
the dogs will be barking outside, the arm of my wonderful

master guards her, embraces her, for the time being dreams
take the place of words, the fires have not been lit, it is cold,
I crouch, I stretch, I am hungry, morning drags its feet, there
are blossoms of ice in the windows, hosts of gray fluffy flakes
are flying, the hour is nigh when they will be white, then
Joseph will depart, whispering to me requests known only to
us, I will rub against his ankles, the moments will be mute,
then, know thou, O queen, I alone will remain here to keep
guard, I try to be pleasing to her, to enliven her, I nudge her
slippers over the floor, I bring from the coat rack the scarf and
the mittens she has knitted, I even push the chamber pot from
under the bed with my paw, I seek lost buttons under the
cupboards, Elena spends most of the time stretched out in the
armchair, she dozes, she toys with the balls of wool, she reads,
sometimes she calls me to sit on her knees and in her lap, she
runs her fingers through my fur, I press my head to her belly, I
count, fifteen kittens are gamboling and scuffling inside.

The child bawled strenuously, like a cat in heat, around an hour and a quarter after midnight. When human calendars had not yet begun that eighth day of March, shortly before noon on the seventh, the tomcat had looked in astonishment at Elena Strauss's dress, stained from the waist down, imagining that his mistress, who had just been cracking eggs for a crème brûlée, had splashed herself with the whites. He hastened to fetch her a cloth, jumping onto the sink and grabbing one in his teeth. Then he coiled like a spring in a corner of the kitchen, his eyes boggling, and it became clear to him what was happening only when Elena staggered to the door, went out onto the landing, and leaned on the banister. Then he streaked between her legs, as if he were chasing a mouse or a rat, he descended like a bolt of lightning, hung with his paws from the handle of the surgery door, swinging there until the handle gave way and, without paying any attention to the fact that Joseph was busy cleaning the canine of a gentleman with dyed sideburns, he leapt onto the dentist's back and mewed in his left ear. Herr Strauss dropped his spatula, stammered something to the startled patient, and ran upstairs, three steps at a time. He was pale, his lips unable to form words, his palms incapable of caresses, and he set off again immediately through the slushy snow, without hat or galoshes, his overcoat unbuttoned, to the house of the old midwife with whom he had consulted many times. And that plump, worldly-wise old woman, whom he had niggled until her hair grew whiter, poring over her midwife's certificate, dressed and prepared without delay, summoning her sister for assistance. Since not only the oaths he had consigned to paper had to be kept but also the promises he had made to Elena in recent weeks, once he had fetched the two midwives Joseph meddled no further. Not even through the keyhole did he watch the events in the bedroom. Throughout the afternoon, evening, and first part of the night, he smoked incessantly, employing all the pipes in his collection, sometimes two, three, or four pipes in as many ashtrays. From time to time he opened the windows wide to fill his lungs and his thoughts with the throbbing frost, and he let his eyes wander over Bucharest. He poured himself apple brandy once in a while, and often set the coffee pot on the stove to boil. He allowed the tomcat onto his chest for a long stretch, stroking him under the chin, talking to him about this and that, not telling him a story, because stories would have meant snatches of the past, instead prophesying and giving vent to a stream of hopes. He told him that mother's milk has the gift of strength, health, and compassion, that it chases away drought and storms, that it always points to goodness and human kindness, just as the polestar points sailors on their way. He confessed that the heart can grow larger and beat madly, leaving the chest and floating away over the world like a balloon. He flattered Siegfried, telling him that his kittens would multiply without number, filling the entire city with their kittens' kittens. He supposed, chewing on his pipe until it almost cracked, that the hair of the newborn child would be chestnut and his eyes blue and haughty. He flattered himself that he, Joseph Strauss, would be strong and redemptive, lifting the baby up to the ceiling, dandling him, and helping him to release his first happy cry.

Some time earlier, when Elena's belly had barely begun to swell, he had in great secret tended to a funeral. This was because he believed that the peace of the newly born depends on those who have ascended to the Heavens, that new shoots can emerge into the light only from the roots, bulbs, or seeds of older plants, that in a new land fate will smile on no one unless he has his own dead in the ground. That summer he had found a crackpot priest and haggled with the gravediggers so they would dig deep; to keep their mouths shut, he had frightened them with the ravages of an unknown contagious disease. One Wednesday evening in the Catholic cemetery, he had taken part in a service officiated in accordance with all the canons. In the two coffins were laid rocks wrapped in layers of white canvas and velour, weighing as much as a human body, and along with them all kinds of sundry items: a pocket mirror, spectacle frames, a handbag with charred edges, a smoke-blackened fan, some tweezers, a pouch filled with a fine powder (a tea that smelled of mushrooms), a parasol, a few letters, photographs, and a pair of amethyst earrings. Engraved on the granite crosses were the names of Gertrude and Irma Strauss, who had come into the world in 1817 and 1838, respectively, and had both joined the ranks of the righteous, according to the inscription, in 1869. Under the circumstances, the true year in which his mother and sister had perished, Anno Domini 1864, could not possibly be carved upon the stone.

And if for that burial, Joseph Strauss had for the first time removed from their hiding place under the floorboards six gold florins, it was from the same place that he also later took, one morning when his wife was out shopping, the diamond ring. He had decided to use it for the good fortune and health of the newborn baby, offering the midwife who was to cut the child's umbilical cord much more than she expected (or dreamed of), and for a quiet but bountiful christening. He had gone to a number of jewelers in the January blizzards and snows, had the ring valued and sold it through one of them, receiving a goodly sum from a carpet merchant, a man with a side parting and a brown wart on his cheek. And indeed he had paid Sevastitza the midwife enough for ten births, but otherwise all had not gone quite as he had imagined. Instead of bursting into the bedroom, embracing his beloved wife and showering her with kisses, cradling the baby and whispering a prayer over him, he had awoken, groggily, from a faint, his forehead gashed on the edge of a cupboard, with the tense faces of the two sisters hovering over him, with the great wonder of the place, moment, and situation in which he found himself, with his heart, as he had predicted to Siegfried, beating madly, about to leave his chest and float through the room that was filled with the exhalations of sweat and dried blood. For hours and hours he had listened to the groans of Elena, he had seen the women coming and going, calling for fresh cloths, wetting their eyebrows with cold water and drinking strong black tea, he had walked for dozens of miles around the room that faced the street, he had numbered thousands of stars in the moonless sky, losing count and then starting over, and after he heard the child's first whine, barely had he been called in and discovered that he had a son than he had collapsed like a limp rag in the doorway. They wafted smelling salts under his nose, they rubbed his temples and wrists with vinegar, and finally the midwife slapped him so smartly that he woke up. For a while he was unable to hop around the room, whoop for joy, dandle the baby at his breast, or kneel beneath the icon and praise the good Lord. All three of them lay in the broad, raft-like bed, with the baby in the middle, ruddy-faced and wriggling, wrapped in a little green blanket, his parents holding hands and gazing deep into each other's eyes. In the middle of the night, after the women had finally ventured to leave (having been awaited in the street for long hours by a stout young lad with a conical fur hat) and after the baby had been placed for the first time in the osier cot, Siegfried softly approached the oval mattress, fearfully inspected the man-kitten, sniffed him and twitched his whiskers, then curled up by his feet and fell asleep. Joseph and Elena, who had decided many times not to let the tomcat near the child, at least for a few months, watched him anxiously at first, then calmly and lovingly. Sleep overcame them. Swiftly.

On the very same day, March 8, 1870, at the morning's end, that helpless little mite, Alexandru Strauss, of the male sex, was recorded as entry no. 214 in the Registry of Births, thanks to the declaration signed by his father, Joseph Strauss, dentist, Catholic, of Lipscani Street, and witnessed by Sevastitza Florian, authorized midwife, of Armenească Lane, and Otto Huer, barber, of Şelari Lane, and to the goodwill, earned with a bribe, of Vasile Tincoviceanu, one of the scribes of the Saint

Nicholas quarter. Afterward, the same as on the evening they had first met, the two Germans went to a tavern and once again lost count of the mugs of beer. With chastened laughter, they discovered over the first mug that the philandering life no longer preoccupied either of them. Over the second or third mug one of them whispered, while the other listened with reverence, all kinds of things concerning newborn babies, not the things women talk about, with their charms against evil, with their swaddlings, lullabies, and old wives' remedies, but different things, such as the fact that a man's soul melts for joy, that droplets of his soul can be seen gleaming on his cheeks and trickling down his chin, dripping onto the baby's delicate skin, that the fine, porous skin slowly absorbs them, until another soul coagulates within the fragile body. Over the fourth or fifth mug, they agreed that the throes of labor and, more importantly, the forging of a dynasty were also in store for the newly wedded wife of Prince Karl, Elisabeth Pauline Ottilie Luise—daughter of Prince Hermann of Wied and goddaughter of the widowed queen of Prussia—with her massive frame, broad, bulging forehead, cheeks like puffy pouches fused to her jawbones, and the good fortune to marry when she had already resigned herself to the life of an old maid. And over another mug, the last, which might well have been the fifth, sixth, or seventh, the dentist confessed that he was suddenly on tenterhooks and had to get home as quickly as possible. They walked, tottering as they went, and, still tottering, they urinated endlessly in a dark passageway, whence they were chased with curses by a seamstress in a headscarf who kept trying to whack them with a rolling pin on the arms, legs, and back. They barely managed to escape, buttoning their flies in haste and soaking the crotches of their trousers.

The christening was held six weeks after the birth, on the next-to-last Sunday of April, the infant being immersed in the font by a young priest with a wispy beard and hesitant movements. Elena Strauss never feared that the priest might drop the child in the lukewarm water, and she felt a kind of pride when Alexandru, after his brief and sacramental bath, piddled on the shirt of his (and their) godfather, Calistrache, who was blinking incessantly. Remembering the episode in the dark passageway, and laughing with the tall cook, Joseph realized that not only had the father's soul come to nestle in the breast of his son, but also the father's habits, both seemly and unseemly. Calistrache had just recited the creed, without stuttering, and the Unclean One had been cast out from the vicinity of the infant, when Elena gave a start, glimpsing by the door a visage with bushy mustaches, another with bluish-white cheeks, and two merry little faces. It had been almost two years since she had seen the boy and girl to whom she had been governess, and as long since she had heard from Theodor Nikolić of Rudna and his wife, Antonija. She had sent the baron and baroness eleven letters, but had received only an icy, obdurate silence for her pains. She had begged their forgiveness, she had spoken to them of passion and tranquility, she had thanked them for the gentle past, she had painted for them a present that often resembled a dizzying dream, she had recounted to them details from a marriage that did not yet know strife, she had never hidden from them that she missed them, she had always asked about the children's favorite sweets and games, about the lady's migraines and about the gentleman's zeal for riding, she had described to them an astounding tomcat with one white ear and one black ear capable of assisting her when she knitted and cooked, and she had confessed that the only bitter thing in her life was their dry, unending anger. All these thoughts had been written and re-written steadfastly, because the man with the bushy mustaches and the woman with bluish-white cheeks, who together had bought her from a wretched village in the Rudnička region when she was only three years old, paying a pauper, Ivailo Duković, four sacks of potatoes, a cow with a full udder, fif-teen bushels of flour, and a gold piaster, were like parents to her, while the little boy and girl had become her siblings, no different than her eight long-forgotten blood brothers and sis-ters. After the service, she took Joseph by the hand, clutched the child to her breast before he could be properly swaddled, and walked to the entrance of the church, coming to a stop before those people who had grieved her for so long. There by the oak door could be divined embraces, caresses, whispers, sighs, tearful voices. Standing apart from the women and chil-dren and clearing his throat, the baron invited the dentist to come play a game of chess and, since the heat of summer was not far off, to share a few glasses of that liqueur with three names, raki, ouzo, and mastika. One evening. Whenever he pleased. Later, in the churchyard with its white and red peo-nies, its daisies, and its thronging crows, surrounded by such a tranquility as can be found in Bucharest only at noon on Sun-days, the Baron and Baroness Nikolić of Rudna showered the child with gifts. As if he were their own grandson.

Ever since Miss Duković had consented to bear the name Strauss there had been, however, one discord between hus-band and wife, never acknowledged or commented upon, a muffled, enduring disagreement that showed no sign of di-minishing. On the Sunday when she had first remained alone on the upper floor of the redbrick house, Elena had carefully examined the mountain landscape on the west-facing wall, she had stroked the bronze frame and the oil paint spread over the canvas, she had rummaged in the lumber room for long minutes, returned with a hammer and nail, climbed onto a stool, and carefully knocked the nail into the wall, moving the painting a hand's width lower and farther to the right. On his return, not right away, but only after dusk began to fall, Joseph noticed that the painting had shifted its position. He said not a word. He waited for her to go into the bedroom and returned the alpine landscape in muted colors to its former place, then followed her between the enticing sheets. Since then, in a silent ritual, each had been hanging the painting on his or her own nail, for half a day at a time. Uninterruptedly.

On Lipscani Street a few hours after sunrise the bustle and din were so great that a man passing that way for the first time would have thrown up his hands in astonishment and most likely fled. Herr Strauss, however, had grown accustomed to the swarming townsfolk and thronging carts, barrows, carriages, and cabs, to the recalcitrant beasts of burden, to the cries of the vendors of kvass, pies, and yogurt, to the elbowing and shoving apprentices, to the swaggering journeymen and slippery-eyed merchants, to the thronged stores, to the ladies lingering in front of shop windows and the gentlemen's hats bobbing above the crowd, to the universal haste, and, above all, to the clouds of flies that would not be driven away by the commotion. He knew very well that in Bucharest he would never find a better spot for his occupation, and he knew equally well that all of those people would prefer to fritter their money away on anything rather than the health of their teeth. At the end of the summer, one Friday, as he was struggling to extract the residual stumps of a molar in his sunlit surgery, he had seen through the window a young woman with a small child clinging to her left hand and a cane in her right. She looked like one more of the hundreds of images that passed before his eyes every morning, and so he paid her no mind, heedful of the pincers and small chisel with which he was working, heaving away at the ruined tooth. Later, after he had washed himself with soap, taken his fee from the bald innkeeper, and recovered from his exertions, he noticed that the woman and her brat had not vanished from the window, but had drawn even closer, as if to shelter from the torrent of passers-by. Before calling a new patient inside, he was able to study them through the translucent curtain, especially since they did not seem to be in much of a hurry. She had a narrow waist, thin arms, and from beneath her yellow headscarf there fell a plait of chestnut hair. He felt a brief shudder, a kind of longing. He placed his hands on his hips, stood on tiptoes, and stretched his joints. He liked the sensation of ease that pervaded his body, and looking at the woman outside he imagined Elena baring her large, milk-laden breasts, offering them to him for kisses, not to the baby to sate its hunger. The child seemed to be a little boy, although he was wearing a girlish linen blouse that fell below his knees. His hair was rumpled like a bunch of hay, he might be two, but perhaps not, and judging from the whitish streaks around his mouth he had been eating halva. He supposed that they must be waiting for someone and that after walking for so long among the crowd they had grown faint and taken shelter by the window. Then, the next patient took his place in the blue velvet chair with one leg in the middle, a lieutenant of the cavalry with an abscess as big as a walnut on his gum. Concentrating on his scalpel, swabs, and the sac of pus, the dentist brushed his elbow against one of the uniform's epaulettes, disturbing the flawless braids and pips. To the accompaniment of muffled groans, stamping the floor with the heels of his boots, and suddenly rearing up like a cock, the officer found the strength to smooth the braids and buff the gold insignia with his fingertips. The doctor compared him in his mind (and soul) with a captain of dragoons from Berlin, who had developed an abscess nearly as large after the chill he had endured on a firing range. He thought with pity of Prince Karl, who had to rein in such an army, such a country, such tantrums. And especially now, when he was reportedly on the point of abdicating, at the end of a very long series of insults and tragicomedies, when the waters of Wallachian politics seemed muddier not only than the Dîmbovitza but all the other rivers and brooks in the land during the rainy season. Measured by how many raindrops fell from the clouds, the year 1870 had been one of drought, but measured by how much muddy water had been splashed about during speeches in the chambers, in the intrigues hatched by the parties, in the attacks published by the newspapers, in the endless quarrels, it might be said that from the outset the skies had opened and turned the earth into a mire. Joseph Strauss was a passionate reader of the newspapers, and, in a single minute—while the cavalry officer straightened his waistcoat and belt, wiped his lower lip with a handkerchief, brushed flecks off his white gloves, sought his wallet, and adjusted his cap—he had recalled how the minister of justice, Boerescu, had been forced to resign because he had had the temerity to propose an annual stipend of 300,000 lei for Elisabeta of Wied, the wife of the sovereign, how the radical liberals had been scandalized and stormed out of parliament on the appointment of Alexandru G. Golescu as prime minister, how that government of straw had come tumbling down in two months, making way for another, of windblown leaves, led by Manolache Epureanu, how Cuza, the erstwhile prince, although he had from his exile categorically declined candidacy as a deputy and then refused the mandate, had nonetheless been elected to the Fourth Congress, how *The Romanian* had railed against the prince, accusing him of wanting to repeal the constitution and rule despotically, how the same rag, on another occasion, suggested him as a model monarch to King Bernadotte of Sweden, how conspiracies and plans to dethrone him were sprouting like weeds in the shadows, how the outbreak of the Franco-Prussian War had inflamed many politicians, providing them with an opportunity to insult the pureblood German prince, how the opposition had, even in excess of their Parisian-scented sympathies, conceived of the absurd demand that the United Principalities should abandon its neutrality through a general mobilization of the army. Finally, as the lieutenant bid him farewell, the dentist smiled, saluted him in military style, and asked whether he thought the events of August 8, in Ploesci, when a handful of men had occupied the prefecture and telegraph office and proclaimed a regency led by General Nicolae Golescu, had been a farcical revolution, a practical joke, a lamentable failure at a coup, a criminal act, a childish game (as Karl Ludwig had called it the following day), or the first, tentative sign of a powerful force hostile to the throne and, in particular, the man on it. But before the lieutenant could reply, or deliver his verdict on the trial in Tîrgoviște, at which rebels with illustrious names — Golescu, Brătianu, Candiano, Carada, Rosetti — were being tried by jury, Joseph had already invited the next patient into his surgery — a rather odd, middle-aged gentleman. He was complaining not of his teeth, but of a host of pustules that had appeared on his belly and back. To soothe him, while attempting to persuade him to visit an apothecary for medicines to suit his ailment, Joseph told him that Princess Elisabeth, too, soon after arriving in Romania, after the religious service at the Metropolia and the civil ceremony in the same place on an open-air dais, had come down with the measles. He was astonished to discover that the woman with the yellow head-scarf and the tousle-haired little boy had not vanished, as he had believed for an hour, an hour and a half, but had merely moved farther to the left, out of the luminous rectangle of the window. As it was getting near lunchtime and no one else had arrived seeking treatment, he took off his physician's coat, washed thoroughly with soap, and rinsed himself at a basin. Out of habit and hunger, he was about to climb the stairs to the upper floor, but he changed his mind and opened the door to the street, remaining on the threshold. Soon, noticing him, the little boy grew embarrassed, thrust his chin into his chest, and seemed to tug his mother by the sleeve. By the way they were dressed and how much time they had wasted outside, Herr Strauss was sure that the woman was going to ask him to take pity on her and to cure her pain free of charge. It was not to be. She turned and gazed in his direction, past his shoulder, blinking slowly, very slowly, staring into space. She was blind. And not only that. It was the blind whore. Linca. He suddenly felt as if his legs had been cut from under him; he could not breathe. He supported himself against the door-frame, then hurried over to the woman and whispered some-thing in her ear. The words of her answer were lost in the sur-rounding din, but Joseph did not wait for them; he led her forward, along the fronts of the buildings, hoping and praying that he had not been seen from the windows of the upper floor at number 18. Then he veered into Șelari Street, stopped at a corner, drew air deeply through his nostrils, and was met with a scent compounded of roast mutton, fried fish, and warm bread. Hunger no longer stalked him, and the mad

beating of his heart had abated. The woman and the little boy
followed him. At every step she tested the pavement with the
toes of her boots and her cane, and they almost toppled over
each other when a lame dog ran in front of them out of nowhere. While they talked, Linca held him by the arm, so that
she would have no doubt that he was there beside her and
that all the words, spoken and unspoken, remained only between them. She showed him the boy, touching the crown of
his head and his cheeks, and asked about that Dutch merchant who, forty months previously, months she had been
counting, had been thrust into her bed. Herr Strauss shrugged,
then realized that his gesture was not worth a penny, and so,
pale as a sheet of paper, he said that he did not know anything, that from what he could recall, vaguely, the merchant
had left Bucuresci in June or July 1867 and that for weeks on
end before he vanished he had been talking of African rubies,
which he was dreaming would make him rich. The woman
smiled a crooked smile and informed him that the Dutchman
had visited her plenty of other times, from May until that
winter, always announcing his arrivals many hours or days be-
forehand, entering by the gate, crossing the graveled path, and
hiding between her sheets in the dead of night, always asking
that the old woman Mareta and the other girls not be at
home, arriving and departing in a carriage that did not creak
or rattle, with horses trained to move soundlessly like cats and
not to snort or neigh. Now it was the dentist who, having
grown dizzy, was leaning on the woman's arm. And she added
that the old biddy had driven her out when her belly had begun to swell, because she had refused to drink green water-
melon tea or boiled wine to induce a miscarriage. She also
told him, without her voice quavering, that she needed to find
the merchant and ask him for money. The hustle and bustle

around the shops had died down somewhat, but Joseph, his mouth agape, did not notice. He took from his waistcoat pocket all the money he had earned in his surgery that Friday morning, and seeking her palm he placed the coins there, large and small, all in a heap. Linca thanked him, coughing and caressing the child's head emphatically.

Whether by chance or not, the next day, which was the twenty-seventh of August, the city's newspapers and gossips took note of the Lord's will. For on that day the good Lord had decided that Maria, daughter of Carol I and Elisabeth, should be born. And born she was.

As Joseph Strauss had been hoping, along with all the other Germans enduring the frosts of the new year, in time not only the snowdrifts, the icy northeasterly wind, the icicles, and the snow storms came to an end, but also the stupid rumors and incessant lies. He had never believed one jot of the news that was concocted on the banks of the Dîmbovitza and that had accompanied from beginning to end the resounding war being waged one thousand miles away on battlefields and maps, in stratagems and, at the same time, in his own heart, which beat passionately for the pennants of Prussia. For weeks on end, every day and even a number of times a day, all kinds of fantastical rumors had reached his ears, rumors that reported as certainties the position of the frontline, the balance of forces, the gains and losses, the morale of the troops, the troop movements, the numbers of dead, wounded, and prisoners, the level of reserve munitions, and, naturally, the predictions of eyewitnesses, who were always knowledgeable, objective, and anonymous. As for King Wilhelm, one of the favorite characters of these winter's tales, now he was supposed to have been hit by shrapnel, now he had broken his leg while beating a hasty retreat, now he had been taken prisoner along with 20,000, 45,000, or 60,000 soldiers. In the same Wallachian whirl of rumor, there was also talk of Ministerpräsident von Bismarck, who was now supposed to be on the brink of losing his mind, having begged the forgiveness and mercy of Gambetta and Trochu in tormented and encrypted letters, now ready to cross the ocean to America with a fortune stashed away in hundreds of trunks, and now in love in his old age with a siren from Lyons, a young maiden in whose palms and between whose breasts he had laid all the military secrets in Berlin. Of all these mad imaginings born by the fireside during the long hours when folk chattered, munched pumpkin seeds (toasted, salted), drank plum brandy (boiled with sugar and pepper) or wine (also boiled, with cinnamon and cloves), counted their money (little), and made children (many), the dentist understood many things, but what he could not comprehend was how such stupidities could be printed on countless pages and peddled to people as the truth. He found no explanation, neither then nor later, and was left merely with the memory of subdued evening chitchat, at the end of which Elena and he, late at night, when the boy was sleeping, would slide under the quilt and forget everything else, even themselves, in kisses and entwinings. In the light of day, however, pallid and short as it was after Epiphany, Joseph saw one thing clearly: that in the frozen city, with its steadfast affection for France, penchant for any Frenchified details and boundless trust in Gallic politics, a madcap wind was blowing, aimed at the sovereign or, to be precise, at Karl Eitel Friedrich Zephyrinus Ludwig, Prince of Hohenzollern-Sigmaringen. And that wind, although it had always blown, now intensified palpably, especially after the huge Strousberg scandal of January 1871, when the Berlin consortium and the Romanian government refused to pay the many, many adventurers, bankers, manufacturers, traders, and ordinary mortals in Prussia who had purchased shares in the railroad of the United Principalities. The theory of the railroad's builder, who had not for one moment renounced the title of doctor or the initials of his forenames, *H* and *B*, had been that upon the provisional opening of the Bucuresci–Buzău–Brăila–Galatzi–Tecuci–Roman section in December '70 it became the responsibility of the Wallachian treasury to honor the coupons and pay its creditors the interest due. On the other hand, it was the opinion of the cabinet, led by Ion Ghika, erstwhile Bey of Samos, once more taken out of peaceful retirement and placed in the prime minister's chair, and the opinion of parliament and Carol I himself that, according to the acts signed by both parties, the financial burden should remain on the shoulders of the concessionaires until the entire railroad network had been completed and irregularities on the newly opened line rectified. The conflict was grist to the mill of the prince's adversaries precisely at a time when water was scarcer and dearer than ever, as the river had turned into a solid floe, resembling a thick white serpent, that stretched from one bank to the other and to both horizons, forcing the water sellers to abandon the holes in the ice they had dug before Christmas and take their sledges far and wide in search of springs that continued to flow. Amid the general uproar, in which the prince had been accused of not having forgotten the source of his blood and of having permanently favored profiteers, embezzlers, and forgers of mortgages, and in which the arrest of all the ministers involved in negotiating the concession, their trial, and the confiscation of their property had been demanded, a joint assembly of the two chambers had voted, feverishly, despite the bitter cold, that the Strousberg affair should be elucidated by a foreign court of arbitration. Saddened and disappointed, perhaps disgusted, not only by those insane attacks but also, as the dentist believed, by the ineptitudes, gaffes, intrigues, and idleness coming in quick succession from the political parties, Karl Ludwig had decided, while the frost was splitting the cobblestones, to tell the public once and for all, gruffly, why his head was splitting. And tell them he did, sending to the *Augsburger Allgemeine Zeitung* for publication a letter nominally addressed to a certain Auerbach, who likely did not exist, but addressed in fact to the whole world, and in particular to those Romanian politicians who had the eyes to see, the ears to hear, and the will not to stand idly by, their arms folded. And the fiery missive, which Joseph had read dozens of times, until it lost its sense and he had learned it by heart, which had been reproduced in other newspapers everywhere and stirred such controversy, began by saying:

> *I should like to see you for but one hour in My place, to assure you of how shattered is my existence and with how many tasks, cares, and deceptions it is filled.*

It was not until halfway through the text that Carol slipped in his view of the real reason for these evils:

> *This ill-fated land, which had always lived under the harshest servitude, went without transition from a despotic Government to the most liberal of constitutions, a constitution such as no other nation in Europe enjoys. I regard this, according to My experience, as a misfortune all the greater given that the Romanians may not be flattered that they possess the virtues of industry . . .*

Joseph Strauss, who understood these words differently than his wife and best friend, Otto Huer the barber, not because he was a more competent interpreter or a more skillful diviner of thoughts, but because he had a different past, chose to be honest to the very end only with Siegfried, who alone knew in what wise the dentist had arrived in Bucuresci and who had invited him thither. And he took Siegfried in his arms one morning, when dawn had not yet scattered the darkness, descended with him into the surgery as if into a frozen grotto, and lit a fire in the stove, which was also like an icy cavern. The doctor listened as the firewood began to crackle, he sat down in the chair with the blue velvet upholstery and the one leg in the middle, shivering and lazing in the spot where his patients trembled, he clasped to his breast the tomcat, wrapped in a towel, stroking him in the way he liked best, tickling him under the chin with his fingertips, and as the dawn broke he read aloud the passages from the letter that had most troubled him:

"If I had not so cared from my heart about the interests of this beautiful land, a land for which in other circumstances the most radiant future might have been foretold, My patience would long since have given out . . ." and "I preserve My freedom to return to My dear fatherland and to lead there, in the bosom of absolute marital felicity, an independent and carefree existence. The strong magnet of the fatherland has never ceased, even in the midst of the difficult trials to which I have been subjected, to exert upon Me its influence. I am sorry only that my good intentions have been disregarded and received with such ingratitude."

Siegfried, with his black ear pricked up and the tip of his tail poking from beneath the cotton towel, had warmed up and was waiting. And the dentist confessed that deep in his soul he sometimes believed that he himself, Joseph, was that fictive Auerbach to whom the prince had addressed his letter. His suspicions were strengthened by the very first sentence: "*I have awaited too long a time to give you any sign of life.*"

As was to be expected, the Strousberg scandal, Carol's blunt epistle, and the course of the Franco-Prussian War had been hardest to swallow for the Liberals, who were now outdoing themselves in their asperity and gestures of hostility toward the throne. Deputy Nicolae Blaremberg had, in his typical fashion, seen fit to claim, in an interpellation in the Chamber, that the sovereign's missive was either apocryphal or an act of high treason, even making a startling allusion to the fate of the Emperor Maximilian of Mexico, who had ended up in front of a firing squad. Another Nicolae, Ionescu, one of the leading factionalists, had proposed in a restricted party meeting that they should bid the prince good riddance, while the newspaper of the radicals, *The Romanian,* had celebrated on February 11, as a barb aimed at the palace, the half decade that had passed since the banishment "*of a Sovereign who violated the Constitution and squandered the public purse.*" In riposte, the prince had been sent from Jassy a long, astonishingly long, list with the signatures of Moldavian conservatives, more than a thousand names, intended as a show of loyalty, an encouragement to him to remain on the throne, and a promise to review the law that had whipped up so many storms, the mother of all laws: the constitution. But for the dentist of number 18 Lipscani Street, for his family, friends, and acquaintances, for all the Germans who lived on that commercial thoroughfare, the surrounding streets, or other quarters of the city, the most important thing was that the winter was on the wane and that the armies of Prussia, the infantrymen, cuirassiers, artillerymen, sappers and buglers, had not taken any account of the buzzing of north Danubian politicians. They could hardly have done otherwise, in fact, because the sound of gadflies droning in the Balkans did not reach as far as the outskirts of Paris, where the ground now quaked under the boom of cannons, the trampling of hoofs, the whizz of bullets, and the clatter of sabers, under the shouts of battle and the groans of the wounded. Truth to tell, maybe one in a hundred of those soldiers had ever in his life heard the name Bucuresci mentioned, and one in ten thousand had any inkling of where it might be. And this geographical ignorance had helped them, as they followed the banners of the black eagle, to inflict a crushing defeat at Sedan, to drive Napoleon III from the throne and from history, to extend the frontiers of the fatherland through the annexation of Alsace and Lorraine, to open the way for the dragoons to march down the Champs Elysées, and to offer Wilhelm I the opportunity to be proclaimed first emperor of Germany at Versailles itself, in a ceremony agonizingly humiliating for the French. As reflected in the mirrors of Bucuresci, which for the most part showed pallid faces, enervated by the ghastly season, the Prussian triumph was noted in grief-stricken terms. *The Romanian* brought out a special edition, with the black borders of an obituary, which announced, referring to the City of Light, that *"the Teutonic hordes are trampling the sacred earth."* On March 10, in the middle of the night, Herr Strauss heard an uproar and the sound of breaking windows. He knew he was not dreaming. He leapt out of bed, quickly closed the bedroom door, so as not to wake Elena and the baby, and looked vigilantly through the curtains of the day room, without lighting a candle. Below, brawlers with torches were shouting slogans against the Germans, reading aloud the shop signs, smashing most of the windows. From the number of torches they were waving, there must have been around forty, and in their fervor it did not occur to them that the Teutonic names might be deceptive, since Germans, Austrians, and Jews all lived in that quarter. They approached swiftly, in small groups, apparently relying on the complete absence of gendarmes. They destroyed everything in their path, first smashing the shutters with clubs and crowbars, then hurling rocks and entering the shops, merrier than if they had been entering a tavern or their own houses. They trod over broken planks and shards of glass as nonchalantly as the dragoons probably strode down the grand boulevard in Paris. They occasionally fired revolvers, there were two or three revolvers, and to Joseph it was clear from the lack of answering detonations that no one was confronting them in the street. And when finally they were confronted, not far from the Zlătari Church, they punched and kicked to the ground the merchant who had dared to stand up to them. If any window was open, they took care not only to smash it to smithereens but also to throw refuse through the gaping hole. Frightened as he had not been for a long time, Joseph thought to call his wife, but there was no need, because the blue Serbian eyes were already there, gleaming in the room, like embers, and her hands clasped his shoulders and squeezed. Elena wanted to boil water and pour it on top of the madmen's heads, and he had to pacify her and beg her to help him with something else. They quickly went downstairs in the dark and picked up the blue velvet chair, managing to drag it into the hall and prop it against the handle of the front door. Before barricading themselves on the upper floor, they gathered, groping in the dark, medical instruments, powders, and liquors. Then all hell broke loose on the ground floor, directly below them. They kneeled by the cot, pressed together, praying to the Blessed Virgin, each according to his and her own language, manner, and creed, for the still sleeping little boy and for each other. The dentist felt the tomcat rubbing against his left thigh and felt ashamed that they had not also prayed for him. And Alexandru, whom they called not Sasha or Alex, but Sănducu, as Sevastitza the midwife had nicknamed him when she knotted his bellybutton, did not stir during all the time the room downstairs was being laid to waste.

As the gang of hooligans left the surgery and, without pausing, turned toward Peter Bykow's bakery, Joseph was able to make out a few faces. They did not seem disfigured by fury or hatred, but rather they glimmered with an oily film of pleasure, an appetite for destruction and humiliation on their cheeks, brows, and chins. Everything concentrated around one face, glimpsed for a second, a familiar face. At the time he did not realize whose outline he was following through the darkness, but the image imprinted itself on Joseph's mind, sinking through millions and millions of dusty images, trying, as in a card game, to find its pair. Later, much later, the *uhlans* made their appearance. They entered on horseback, at the western end of the street, from the direction of Podul Mogoşoaiei, when most of the windows were in pieces and most of the shops ransacked, when those hotheaded louts had already reached the other end of the street, by New Saint George. The cavalry charge was pointless, except, perhaps to make the residents of the street, awake one and all, regardless of tribe, age, religion, or length of nose, shudder and shiver once more. But the louts legged it, vanishing into narrow alleys, passageways, and courtyards. Soon afterward, while the Strausses were assessing the damage by the light of eleven candles, they found Jakob Vogel in their surgery, white as paper, his glasses splotched and crooked, sitting in the only chair left intact, covered in crumbled plaster and asking for a glass of water. He was trembling. He had been coming home from what should have been a great banquet held by the German community of Bucharest in honor of the Emperor Wilhelm, a splendid party but one which a dentist, a barber, a baker, and others, although thinking of the emperor and loving him, had not permitted themselves to attend, leaving their young families at home. And Herr Vogel, who had started to come around after the sips of water and the brown powder administered to him in a teaspoon, related that nothing had gone according to plan, that the discussions and toasts had rambled, that the platters of the first course had barely arrived when the meal had been interrupted, that the music had stopped even before it could start, that his heart had been beating so loudly at one point that in order not to hear it he had started banging the drum abandoned by the tawny-haired musician hiding under the piano, that before eight o'clock, when the ball was due to commence, the Slătineanu Rooms had been surrounded by a motley mob, among whom could be spotted deputies from the camp of the radical liberals and a few elegant youths, perhaps university or gymnasium students, but which otherwise consisted only of tattered wretches, apprentices, and all kinds of idlers, rounded up from the Calicilor slums or who knows where. And some of those hotheads had climbed up into the bell tower of Sărindar Church, clambered up the ropes, and tolled the bells. The chimes had egged on the others to smash the few street lamps, to hurl cobblestones—this being the city's only cobbled street—at the lower- and upper-story windows, to storm the entrance and shout vile slogans, such as "Death to the Prussians!" "Long live the French Republic!" and "To the palace!" Some thirty of the more burly ones had even managed to burst inside and tussle with the guests. Consul-General Radowitz, said Jakob, had proposed that they remain in the building and hold out together, making barricades from tables and chairs, wielding knives and forks not for the feast but for defense, and this had saved many from serious injury or, God forbid, death. During all that time, just as on Lipscani Street, not a single gendarme showed his face, proof that the prefect of police tacitly condoned what was happening. There, too, it was the army that had restored order, the soldiers appearing two hours before midnight, dispersing the mob and occupying the streets leading to the palace. After the optician rose to his feet, smoothed his black overcoat, which was exceedingly rumpled and dirtied, and departed, Joseph and Elena hung a blanket in the empty window frame, hammering it in place, no longer caring about the fresh paintwork.

During Lent, the floorboard in the kitchen beneath which Herr Strauss kept hidden a pouch for pipe tobacco was pulled up once more. And with the guldens and groschen extracted from therein, among the last, he was able to paint and furbish his surgery yet again, ordering new, not overly expensive instruments from Vienna, anatomical charts similar to the ones that had been ripped to shreds, and three pharmaceutical substances that had always been lacking at the apothecaries' shops in Bucharest. He called in a poor handyman, not a professional parquet-layer, to wax the scuffed floorboards, stain the woodwork, and clean the ceiling paneling. He bought a cuckoo clock to replace the smashed pendulum clock, from which springs and cogs spewed like brass guts. And he did not replace the Anatolian carpets on the wall, because a man counts his money differently when he has a child to raise and a wife to keep. In Easter Week, on the Wednesday, after neither he, nor Elena, nor the boy had touched meat for many weeks, Joseph set out for the Scaune district, where the butchers made their living. He was looking for a suitable lamb, from which his dear Serbian wife might cook everything she had been dreaming of: lamb borscht, lamb stew, roast leg of lamb, and her minced lamb and vegetable pie, which she had extolled long ago, on the banks of the Danube. What about a Lenten compote, Joseph had added, laughing, after listening to the menu, earning himself a rebuke, then her laughter. He went into seven or eight places just so that he could gawp at all that was laid out on the counters and at how the cleavers and the knives whirled above the bloodied chopping blocks. In the last shop whose threshold he crossed, as he was sizing up some offal he saw a strapping young man emerge from the door at the back. He was wearing a long apron of buffalo hide and carrying six freshly skinned yearling lambs over his shoulders. Joseph took a step back and froze. It was that young, burly man whose face had gleamed one night by torchlight. He went out, lit his pipe in the middle of the lane, and recalled that he had been in that shop once before, one autumn. Then he went back in, and with a satisfaction that he could barely contain he had the young man weigh the fattest lamb and chop it into pieces, after which he changed his mind and left without buying it. He paid no heed to the uproar in his wake and headed straight to Otto Huer's barbershop, where Peter Bykow and Jakob Vogel, summoned by an apprentice, soon joined them. As there were no customers waiting for haircuts or shaves, they locked the door, pulled down the shutters, and conferred. They agreed first of all that the Resurrection was of higher significance than people and their deeds, and that nothing could be committed during Holy Week, when joy is the sole purpose of things. Proceeding from the description of the beast and the territory of his lair, Peter the baker managed to find out, as the first warm breezes were beginning to blow, that the monster who had devastated Lipscani Street was a butcher's apprentice and that he dwelled in the yard behind the shop, alone, in a small house with a shingle roof and no porch. Then Otto, taking advantage of his scissors, razors, shaving brush, and combs, but also the geniality of that fat customer of his who was wont to laugh at everything—Vasile, the warden of the Colţei Tower—obtained permission for all four of them to climb the narrow spiral staircase any time they liked, to try out their apparatus from the top of the tallest building in Bucharest. They had devised a mute and docile device, which would administer justice in the world. It remained only for Jakob, rummaging in his workshop and attic in search of magnifying glasses and lenses, inventing and constructing, to perfect the mechanism that, even if it was not to bring him laurels and rewards, would at least salve their hearts and allow them to sleep peacefully. And before the beginning of June, Vogel the optician revealed the extent of his skill, bringing to perfection, according to sketches and calculations made over many nights, that simple yet intricate system whereby the rays of the sun would be snatched from the air by a mirror, bound together like blades of wheat through a polished and concave disk of glass, and launched into the distance with magnified strength and masterful precision, having first traversed another seven glass disks of descending size, all slightly convex. The others marveled. Then they waited. And, when the great Midsummer Fair opened, when it seemed that the whole city had migrated there, when all the butchers to a man had plunged into that boundless market, viewing, selecting, and haggling for cattle, when the burghers had locked up their shops and together with the servants left their houses and courtyards deserted, just then, before noon on a cloudless day, from the walkway of the Colţei Tower, a slender streak of light shot out, stopping on the slope of a roof and remaining there unwavering. It was the roof of a small house with no porch, in the Scaune district. They waited patiently once more. And in a few minutes the fire broke out.

7 ✣ Hurried Times

THEN TIME NO LONGER flowed like a sluggish and evil-smelling river, but all of a sudden acquired a different cadence, like the gallop of thoroughbred colts, like the flight of crows fleeing the rains or even the hurtling of locomotives over the plains, where they are not obliged to apply the brakes. Trains had begun to circulate fairly extensively around the country, eliciting delight everywhere. Before the grand inauguration of the Tîrgovişte Station and the official opening of the lines linking Bucuresci first to Piteşti, then to Ploiesci, Buzău, Brăila, Galatzi, Tecuci, and Roman, in the north another three routes had been put into use, amid pomp and ceremony: Paşcani–Jassy, Vereşti–Botoşani, and Roman–Iţcani. And given how extensive the railroad was, how many settlements were dotted along its length, how much boredom accumulated in the flowering plum bushes, how much curiosity collected in drawing rooms and salons, how rarely the chained dogs barked, and how the appetite for courtesies, flirtations, and barbed remarks sharpened in that dusty air, it had become the custom in all of those towns, large and small, that at noon the railroad stations would be assailed by the beau monde, who would watch who boarded and alighted from the carriages and note how a handsome mechanic had waxed his mustache, how the conductor's uniform had been brushed and ironed, how the wheels screeched as the train came to a halt and how they creaked as it departed, and what familiar faces could be glimpsed in the windows. The suspension of the Strousberg concession had been quickly forgotten and, in spite of protests from Berlin diplomats and stern letters signed by Bismarck (no longer merely *Ministerpräsident* of Prussia, but chancellor of the German Empire), those hundreds of miles of track were treated as a gift that had fallen like meteorites from the heavens onto the map of the United Principalities. As for the controversial coupons or, to put it another way, payments of dividends to shareholders, the matter had been taken over by the New Company of Romanian Railroad Shareholders. But the rhythm of the times had not changed on just any day or in any old way, like someone taking off a dirty shirt and putting on a clean one, but had quickened on that rebellious night between March 10 and 11, 1871, when Prince Carol, livid with anger, smoking incessantly and about to come to the boil, had decided to abdicate. First of all, he had demanded the resignations of Ion Ghika and the entire cabinet, and he had summoned to the palace the members of the former Princely Lieutenancy, to hand back the very reins of power he had received from them. Then he had agreed, after countless discussions, consultations, and entreaties, to grant parliament a final, very brief, recess, so that it might clarify its intentions and principles. Satisfied by the dénouement of the secret session in the Chamber and by the panic sown among the parties, he had seen with his own eyes for the first time a solid, coherent, and authoritative government form, led by Lascăr Catargiu, the man who had answered, *"Majesty, this cannot be!"* when he announced that he would be leaving Bucuresci for good. And just as the sun peeps through the clouds at the end of a storm, just as a gentle breeze begins to blow after frosts and icy northeasterlies, just as tranquility returns to the world after the fury of the elements, so too the life of Carol I brightened when he was least expecting it. The Turkish troops massed along the Danube missed the opportunity to cross the river and bring order to a vacant throne, the political adventurers realized how close to disaster they had come, they shivered and cringed like curs at the master's feet, and His Beatitude Metropolitan Nifon begged forgiveness of the city's German community in his own name, that of the Orthodox priesthood, and on behalf of the faithful flock. In April, Karl Ludwig and Elisabeth Pauline were showered with flowers and reverences in Jassy, and in June the royal couple were bathed in affection and loyalty at the elections. In August, they both felt the damp proximity of the Cotroceni marshes and withdrew for a few weeks to Sinaia Monastery. In October, they applauded the large domestic loan obtained by the government, 75,000,000 lei, as a sign of confidence and devotion on the part of the native magnates. Then the one-thousand-eight-hundred-and-seventy-first year, by calendar reckoning, came to a close. In the two years that followed, time continued its hectic flight. In 1872, the German banks of Bleichröder and Disconto-Gesellschaft financed the extension of the railroad to the Austro-Hungarian and Russian borders, trade blossomed like robinia or at least like chamomile, Princess Elisabeth was cured of malaria in Italy, and Prince Carol hunted bears and boars in the Peleş Valley. That autumn, waves of astonishment washed over the city when, on the site of a stagnant pool by Liberty Fields, a huge structure was erected, described in the newspapers as "*Bucuresci's source of light, the forever blessed Gas*

Works," and when sixty miles of cables snaked beneath the earth, and four thousand gas lamps were lit at nightfall, on streets, in squares, in public parks, and by vacant lots. By 1873, the schools and law courts were hobbling less, the first broad boulevard appeared, running past the university and linking Podul Mogoșoaiei with Colței Lane, the royal palace was entirely renovated, shedding its shabby, provincial air and bluish-gray plaster, new docks and warehouses were built in the Danube ports; and Carol I and Elisabeth traveled abroad, stopping off at Vienna, where they visited the World Exposition and met Emperor Franz Joseph at Erms for talks with Tsar Alexander, then stayed at some of the prince's ancestral castles and finally Ilmenau, an oasis of indulgence and health. As was their good custom, they spent dozens of days in Sinaia, residing in the monastic cells, gazing at the mountain crests and boundless forests, seeking the ideal spot for a future summer palace, carefully examining the plans drawn up by the architect Doderer, and playing for hours on end with the little Princess Maria, who, given all the languages she was learning and all the teachers that were cramming her head, had mangled the English *little* and come to be called Itty.

Naturally, the new tenor of the times did not bypass Lipscani Street or the redbrick building at number 18. In the dwelling on the upper floor, Joseph was much busier than in the past; he ate in haste, as if he always had business that could not wait, even between the sheets he was changed, forgetting tenderness and enamored whispers in his rush to reach that secret place, hidden beneath black, crinkly Serbian hair, a place whence, he did not doubt, sprang a part of the wonder of the world. Elena, in her turn, no longer strove to make every stew, pilaf, roast, pudding, or pie a miniature work of art. She was frightened by the thought that, however much she might wish for it and whatever she might do, her belly would never swell again. At first when she realized that no new soul was nestling in her womb, she had listened to the counsels of the dentist and plunged into bodily pleasures and love, but when that failed she had done the rounds of priests, quacks, and physicians, who had mystified her with strange services, strict fasts, and hundreds of genuflections, with powders made from grasshoppers' legs, beech mast, ducks' beaks, clay, kids' horns, and cuckoos' eggs, with potions of unknown roots, leaves, and flowers, and with a host of pagan charms that caused her to shudder. She showered all her pampering on the boy, who had long since ceased to gurgle, toddle, piddle in his nappy, and seek the teat, preferring now to suck his right thumb. She had tried every way to wean him from this bad habit, not scolding him, but pleading with him, sprinkling his thumb with ground pepper, paprika, and ash, dipping it every hour in vinegar, fish oil, and quinine. In the end she had left him in peace with his great passion, which he did not renounce even when offered sticks of barley sugar: holding them in his left hand, he would lick them joyfully and insatiably, but then all of a sudden he would remember his thumb and clamp it between his lips. Herr Strauss teased his son, claiming that he had never yet come across a judge, officer, postman, or carpenter who kept his thumb in his mouth all day long. Perhaps that was why, he would add, pipes and cigarettes had been invented, so that men would not make fools of themselves. Joseph and Elena doted on Sănducu. They crawled around on all fours neighing while he rode their backs like a cavalryman on the attack, they hid around the house, called to him, and when he found them they covered his cheeks in kisses, they imitated a multitude of animals and birds, bleating, cheeping, roaring, growling, grunting, lowing, and barking, transforming the house into a menagerie and making the tomcat mew at the top of his lungs, they discovered to their amazement that some games were Serbian, German, and Wallachian all at the same time and they slowly, slowly recalled their rules and rituals: one of them would be blindfolded with a scarf and try to catch the others, they chose to be an *uhlan,* sergeant, or hunter and chase the pigeons, thieves, or ducks, they pretended to be stone statues, waiting to see who would be the first to blink or flinch, they built castles from colored building blocks, they drew, sang, talked with the dolls, and sometimes they tossed an apple-red ball at yellow and green skittles. In the evenings, Otto Huer often demonstrated his peerlessness as a magician. The barber would wave his arms and mutter unfathomable words, he would watch how the small blue eyes grew large and bright, how the wavy chestnut hair quivered, how the pale little face flushed, he would make a broad, sweeping gesture and pull something out of his hat or sleeve, from under his coat or his trouser folds. Then with a deep bow and the endearment *"kleiner König!"* he would place in the outstretched palms a spinning top, a whistle, a jumping jack, a horsie, or a wooden sword. Sometimes he would produce halva, fondants, or pistachio cakes, but then would have to face the reproaches of Joseph, who did not allow the boy to eat sweets before bedtime. Similarly, when his conjuring tricks brought to light noisy playthings, such as a tin trumpet, a rattle, and a circus drum, Elena Strauss would narrow her lips and look at him reprovingly, knowing that the barber was trying to delight the boy and to tease her in equal measure. But in those hurried and good years irritations passed quickly, and once Sănducu had been put to bed they would pour out schnapps and talk about everything under the moon and stars. Their conversations were priceless to Siegfried, who, on many of the barber's visits himself received a visit from the peerless cat, Ritza, as humans called her, Manastamirflorinda by her real name, who would arrive in a wicker basket like his own, the choicest of she-cats, with flecks in her fur like burning coals, with her sinuous walk and particular way of whispering to him and soothing him. At nightfall the tomcat would sprawl on the floor, dizzy, his warm muzzle seeking her wet one, and in the morning as he stretched in the same place on the floorboards, he would silently suffer the child's teasing, always assuming, whenever he was pulled by the tail, by his white or black ear, by his paws or whiskers, that the gesture showed friendship, not malice. In the afternoon hours, Siegfried would laze on the windowsills in the sun when Sănducu was out for a walk, exploring the large, bustling city, its lanes, its horses and carriages of every variety, its crows and ring doves, its single broad cobbled avenue, its motley crowds, its stray dogs and its rooftop cats, its shop windows, hats, spires, and belfries, its new boulevard and two magnificent parks—Cişmigiu and Bishopric, where his parents often took him. In the second of these he would run by himself down the lanes to the column in the center, which seemed to him terribly high, as he threw his head back and gazed for long minutes at the eagle on the top. He was not interested in who had carved it, even though it had been a German, Karl Storck, but he did want to know when he would be able to climb to the top, to clamber on the back of the stone bird. He asked this question so passionately that he did not notice that his lisping voice spoke now Romanian, now Serbian, now German. He had learned all three languages at the same time, because that was how they told him his bedtime stories.

The fresh and untiring breeze that still blew through the United Principalities (along with the icy northeasterly *krivec*,

the dry southwesterly *austru,* and the warm southerly *băltăreț*)
also filled the dentist's sails, making his occupation rise in esteem and the pennies jingle more merrily in his purse. There
had not been any miracles, but things had begun to go well
for him. There were plenty of patients to be found in his waiting room, and the chair with the blue velvet no longer sat
empty except in the rare moments when Herr Strauss was
catching his breath. He had not yet gone on to delicate work,
such as gold molars and incisors (as he would have wished),
but he was content with Bucharest's newly adopted custom
of treating its decayed teeth. He kept a daily reckoning in a
ledger with brown covers, wrapped in silk, taking care not to
record the entire profits of any given day but only five sixths,
and putting aside the rest of the money in a waxed envelope
that he kept hidden behind the shelves that held his medical instruments. As for the tobacco pouch under the eighth
floorboard from the door in the kitchen, he had not touched
it for two years and hoped not to have to do so any time
soon. It still contained three florins, a gulden, and five groschen, but it was as if he had forgotten those yellow coins,
preoccupied only with those of silver and copper. He was always afraid that Elena might find out about the secret money
and he had at the ready a number of explanations: that the
bribes demanded by the pen pushers were large, that money
put aside never hurt anyone, that a lady's coat with an ermine
collar was expensive, or that he was planning a trip to a spa,
their first holiday together. He knew that he loved her more
than he had ever imagined he could love anyone and he also
knew that the secret to which he alone was party, a secret as
large as a hundred secrets, capable of demolishing a throne, of
rocking the city and shattering marriages, must never reach
her ears. And the hurrying times had also caused the girl with

chestnut hair, the blind whore who said she was no longer a whore, to turn up more and more often and to make ever greater demands. She had first reappeared outside the surgery window six weeks after her initial visit, dragging the tousle-headed little boy by the hand and asking insistently where the Dutchman lived. Joseph, on catching sight of her, did not wait until lunchtime. As ever, he fell for her ploy. He went limp, then hastily went out, with the aim of leading her far away. In a narrow passageway, by the Şerban Vodă inn, he gave her money. He begged her not to seek him out again and swore to her that he no longer had any dealings with the merchant or any idea of his fate. A month later, however, on a day of drizzle, he saw her again at the window on the street and this time he was overcome not only with faintness but also with fury. He wanted to speak to her curtly, threateningly, but before he could open his mouth, in that passageway which reeked of piss and whose shadow would have seemed the sun itself to her eyes, he felt something being stuffed into his hand. Linca whispered to him to look carefully, and he, Joseph Strauss, spread out the soft white cloth, smoothed it with his fingertips and could not tear his eyes away from the monogram. He recognized the insignia of Karl Eitel Friedrich Zephyrinus Ludwig, Prince of Hohenzollern-Sigmaringen, former captain of dragoons, middle son of Prince Karl Anton, husband of Elisabeth Pauline Ottilie Luise of Wied, father of Maria, the little princess (who preferred to be called Itty), and sovereign over five million souls. In his stomach, chest, and mind there arose a craving to drink some strong liquor, in great quantities and immediately. He begged her not to leave, and glancing at the child as he went, ran to the adjacent inn, crossed the huge courtyard, entered the tavern, and tossed back, one after the other, three glasses of plum brandy. Afterward, returning to the woman, he wanted to know who else had examined the handkerchief, how old the boy was, and where they lived. Her answers cleared up all but the final question, for he was unfamiliar with the streets of the Calicilor district. He did not give her so much as a brass farthing then, but he promised her that they would meet the following day, in the churchyard of Saint Catherine's at the third hour after noon, to settle a number of matters. While Elena and Sănducu were sleeping, he left a note on the table explaining that he would be away for an hour or two, that he had gone to attend to a Dutch merchant who was wracked with pain, and that he kissed them tenderly. Beneath a shady linden, on a bench, he came to an agreement with Linca that he would give her money every fortnight, a sum on which she could live decently and look after the child. The boy was called Petre. He was five years old, had a slightly hooked nose, prominent but not jagged cheekbones, and eyebrows that by all indications would turn out to be bushy. On the seventh or eighth meeting, in the snow, under the now bare linden, the girl grasped his arm and offered him her body. Whenever and however. He refused her.

As was to be expected, the six chairs in the day room, formerly upholstered in yellow velvet, then in plush the color of milky coffee, were once again in a lamentable state. The tomcat had required not four years to scratch, score, and shred them, but only one, especially since during that year, which he, with his feline powers, had named the Year of the Baby, no one had paid any attention to his psalms, as all the eyes in the house were fastened upon the suckling infant. When the young Serbian woman awoke as if from a long, deep sleep and looked around her, reclaiming dominion over each object and attending to each little detail, the backs of the chairs began once more to disturb her peace of mind. She had gone out one afternoon, while Joseph and Sănducu were building a kite from reeds and paper, with a tail of glossy red ribbons, and she had scoured the shops of Lipscani and the surrounding streets. She had asked to see hundreds of bolts of cloth, had felt materials and gauged their thicknesses, made up her mind and changed it countless times. Wearied by so much walking, dizzied by so many shades, patterns, and prices, and so many discussions with vendors, she had ended up drinking a mug of kvass and going home. It was not until she was preparing some French beans, rinsing them and leaving them to soak, that she made her choice. The next day, as the beans were boiling on the hob with some bacon, onion, and spices, she set out with the child in her arms, and without tapping on the door at the bottom of the stairs or saying a word to the dentist she went straight to Covaci Street, to a Greek trader, from whom she purchased forty feet of thick canvas, the color of mustard or yellow pears. By the end of the week, the six chairs had been clad in covers she herself had sewn, with tasseled edges.

Three years later, in March 1874, on the twenty-ninth day of the month, it happened that those sturdy chair covers, on which the tomcat did not like to sharpen his claws, were taken off and left to soak. Siegfried was alone in the house and once more he came upon the old coffee-colored plush. On one of the chair backs, among the other poems, he found a smooth, narrow patch, and at once set about writing.

(cat year fourteen thousand four hundred and twenty-one, month of Entwined Frogs, twelfth day)
Listen to me, thou, O queen, listen to me and be mindful, my master turned white as chalk and his voice choked, he kept

reading the rumpled newspaper, he did not close it, he did not
leaf through it, he sat slumped in an armchair, with his back
stooped, with his head bowed, with his head in his hands, he
paced in a daze, I could not count his paces, nor how many
times he sighed, he leaned against the window frame and
gazed at the darkling sky, he did not look at the rooftops, at
the birds, at the plumes of smoke or the clouds, through the
darkness sometimes flit spirits and secrets, the darkness spoke to
us, but it could not perceive us, the sadness whirled, whistled,
thickened, I did not count his silences, nor how often he
blinked, my master clutched his son in his arms, tousled him,
caressed him, whispered to him, in the room it seemed hot and
cold, seven candles flickered, Joseph took off his coat and sat
down, I could hear something ticking ceaselessly, it was not the
clock, nor was it the gilded pocket watch, I understood all at
once what that ticking was, he unbuttoned his shirt, his heart
was racing! Know thou, my love, that his eyes were soft and
watery, Elena touched his shoulders, his crown, his temples,
she pressed his brow to her belly, to her beautiful breasts, tears
trickled down my master's cheeks and his voice quavered, he
was saying gloomy things, incessantly, words that hid among
the folds of her dress or remained unspoken, smoldering; he
had read in the newspaper that a little girl had died, was
he then crying only in pity? I could not count his secrets, nor
how many times he lit his pipe, the tobacco burned gently, the
night did not drive away my fear, I would give my soul for
Joseph, may thou forgive me, I rubbed against his ankles and I
jumped into his lap, may thou not scold me, he kept twitching,
starting, I thought of all our kittens, fifty-three, might any
of them have passed away? I, too, sensed the taste of grief, I
stretched out on his breast, I comforted him, I sank into terrors
as if into aspic, I yearn for thee, my love!

On the morning when Siegfried squeezed his new psalm in among his older texts, Joseph and Elena Strauss set out early toward Cotroceni, after leaving the boy at the baker's house. Their hired carriage proceeded with difficulty, because the road, as far as the eye could see in both directions, was crowded with other somber conveyances, moving in single file. The horses advanced at a patient walk, occasionally stopping and then going on, and they were constantly being overtaken by people dressed and shod in every possible manner, all of them heading to the monastery church of the royal residence. Over the bridge, on the banks of the Dîmbovitza, where the vehicles had slowed to a snail's pace, Joseph paid the coachman and they decided to alight. They held each other by the hand, so as not to lose one another in the throng. They were silent, and silent they remained as they climbed the gentle slope, careful at first as to where they trod, but then no longer mindful of their boots and clothes. They walked slowly, borne along by the stream of people, and so it took them more than an hour to cover the short distance. Above, in the garden of the Princess Elena Orphanage, thousands of souls had gathered on one side of the church, at a distance, where they hoped to hear snatches of the service carried on the wind. The little Princess Maria, who had called herself Itty, had fallen ill on Easter Sunday, in that very place, playing with the orphans, running and laughing. The scarlet fever had consumed her and taken her away to the angels. Her laughter was never more to peal in the United Principalities or anywhere on this earth. Her sufferings had dissolved in a place of greenness and tranquility. Her face was no longer rosy, but thereafter, at least in the month of May, the color of the peonies would recall her cheeks. Now the human languages, as many as she had learned, crumbled to dust in Paradise, where the children learn a single language, that of the Heavens. By noon, with his shoulder pressed to the shoulder of his wife, lost in the gray multitude, Joseph did not feel the water in his boots, or the damp air, or the biting cold. He thought of the little girl with the blue dress, lying under so many veils. He also thought of her father, and he kept trying to glimpse the face of the prince. As the little coffin was lowered into the grave, he caught only a vague, distant outline, a flash of a general's uniform. In the afternoon, after two hours of waiting, when they at last reached the grave, his hazel eyes read what was written on the cross. Inscribed in two lines, it went like this: *Maria* and *Christ is risen!*

It was autumn 1875, and the uproar that had burst out on Whitsunday, when the royal train had been involved in a serious accident near Bucharest and Carol I had miraculously escaped from the mangled iron girders, and panels with only a superficial wound below one knee, had long since died away. Quite some time had passed, too, about eight weeks, since the laying of the foundation stone of Peleş Castle in Sinaia, when the prince with his own hand had grasped the trowel and smoothed the mortar, praying not only for the new building but also for the birth of a dynasty. And in the middle of October, one evening, drinking red wine and chatting, Herr Strauss finally understood that Karl Ludwig's prayer that August had referred to the fruit of Elisabeth Pauline's womb. Above and beyond the gossip of the town, which had been saying for years that the princess was barren, Joseph had just heard from his friend Otto Huer that she was paralyzed, the result of a nerve disease. He tossed back his glass and quickly refilled it; he listened for further details, but found they were no more than harebrained rumors, and so he changed the subject, smiled, and beneath that smile concealed his suffering and regrets. He admonished himself for not having told Otto over their very first beer how he had arrived in that city. He was sorry that he had not spoken to him of his visits to the palace, of the powdered *Amanita muscaria,* and, above all, of the blind whore. His heart truly ached in his chest for having hidden from Elena so many things: the prostitutes, his connection to the prince, and, from start to finish, the subsequent nightmare, in which there was nonetheless a glimmer of light, the little face of an innocent child with a slightly hooked nose and increasingly bushy eyebrows, who was called Petre. He poured himself some more wine, not once, but four times, and after the barber left to go home, while Elena and Sănducu were breathing peacefully, asleep in the next room, he called the tomcat, the only one who knew everything. He took him in his arms and stroked him for a long time. He saw in the darkness how the tuft of white fur at the tip of his tail moved slowly, rhythmically, like a lazy pendulum. The next day, he shut up his surgery earlier than usual, and before lunch, telling his wife he had some business to attend to, he went out into the bustling street, veered off along narrow lanes, and walked for a brief space along the boulevard, then down Podul Mogoşoaiei, raised his hat to acquaintances, did not look at the buildings, or at the clouds, passed by the palace, and came to a stop on the southern side of the guardhouse. Presenting all kinds of documents, which attested to his medical studies, his places of employment in Prussia, his Berliner origins, and the fact that he was now a dentist in Bucuresci, he demanded an audience with Prince Carol. The officer who kept the register studied the documents carefully, although he seemed not to understand German. He looked at Joseph a number of times and said that he would be informed of the response at home, by letter.

In early January, when the city was still hung over after the feast of Saint Basil and preparing for the frosts and wassails of Epiphany, at his door Joseph found a military courier, who made him sign for an envelope. On the sheet of paper within, beneath the signature of the marshal of the royal household, Theodor C. Văcărescu, he was informed that he, Joseph Strauss, German, Roman Catholic, dentist, residing on Lipscani Street at number 18, was to be received by H. H. the Prince on Thursday, January 14, 1876, at ten minutes to five P.M., sharp. He took the announcement as a gift, if not divine, then at least propitious. Especially since the day it arrived, the eighth of the month, was his fortieth birthday. Later, when Thursday came at last and the calendar showed the number 14, he entrusted himself to Otto Huer for a shave and haircut. He obeyed Elena to the last detail with respect to clothes, shoes, and handkerchief, and when Sănducu placed a four-leafed clover in his palm, he slipped the lucky charm into his waistcoat pocket. After explaining to them one last time what he wanted to petition the prince about, a complicated matter of taxation, he put his right foot forward when he crossed the threshold, and hailed a horse-drawn cab. As required, he arrived at the royal palace half an hour before the audience. He left his coat, galoshes, and kidskin cap in the cloakroom, and then he was led by a lackey, not the doorman in livery or the Arab butler with the shalwars and turban, into the waiting room next to the adjutants' office. As he made his way across the broad vestibule, the interior no longer seemed familiar. Huge oriental carpets were stretched over the parquet, oil paintings with views of Istanbul hung on the walls facing the chancellery offices, landscapes from the Principalities hung on the other side, and at the foot of the stairs, behind a glass partition curtained with purple velvet, were two life-sized bronze wolves. In the room he entered, there were four other men, including a grain merchant and a former minister of justice, a pale man from the faction of the moderates. The air was not stifling, but the minutes sizzled, glowed, flickered like hot coals. A number of times, the dentist felt the need to loosen the knot of his cravat and to open the top buttons of his shirt, but he refrained and instead sat with his legs crossed, examining his shoelaces. He thought that his meeting with Karl Ludwig would resemble a strange confessional, in which each would shrive the other and confess his own sins. However it might be, he was sure that he, Joseph, would leave that discussion relieved, having rid himself of somber dreams and fears. He tried to guess whether he would be received in the office, in the library, or in some newly furbished room. He wondered whether between the bookshelves he would still find the collection of old weapons and, in particular, the unusual portrait of Erlkönig, the prince's beloved stallion. When the door opened, he was called in first. He took a step toward the stairs, supposing that they would be ascending to the upper floor, but the functionary checked him with an admonitory whisper and showed him into a room on the other side of the hall. In the office of the marshal of the royal household, the dentist was heard for a quarter of an hour by a mere counselor. He mumbled something vague about taxes being too high and about the gifts demanded by the men from the treasury. Through the monocle fixed upon him could be discerned a disbelieving—and bored—pupil.

The times continued to hurry, streaking like rabbits or soaring like hawks. In the same way, for example, as the new liberal coalition. First it emerged from the egg, then grew strong and learned to flap its wings in the house of Mazár Pasha (who, to cap it all, was in fact a Briton of Dutch origins, Sir Stephen

Bartlett Lakeman, former commandant of a death squad in South Africa, a veteran of the Crimean War, and a mercenary in the service of the sultan), wheeled for months and months high in the political sky, stalking its prey, before swooping ruinously upon Lascăr Catargiu, toppling him from power. In April, after five years without significant crises or reversals, the Principalities were left with a strange council, which the newspapers christened the Ministry of the Sword, because it was led by General Ioan Emanuel Florescu and included another two career soldiers, with braided bands down their trousers. It was also in April, after the life of the first transition cabinet had proven more ephemeral than a summer midge, that the ever present Manolache Costache Epureanu took his seat in the prime minister's chair. In July, he was obliged to get up again and leave for his estate, where he could better bear the summer heat. Taking his place at the head of the government, after some three thousand five hundred days, bitterly long days during which he had dreamed of nothing else, was the 'Vizier.' And Ion C. Brătianu lived up to his nickname. After winning renown for having supposedly taken part in a plot against Napoleon III, after accompanying a captain of dragoons from Berlin to Bukarest to see him elevated to the throne, after striving to manipulate the prince from behind the scenes, after being the first minister of war not to hold the rank of officer, after thundering and fulminating against the sovereign from the benches of the opposition, after plunging himself up to his neck in the ridiculous Ploesci revolution, after donning sackcloth and ashes and kissing the hand he had tried to bite, and many other provocative escapades and episodes, he had got it into his head at the height of the dog-day weather, when the year 1876 blazed like an oven, to attempt from his position as president of the council to arrest all twelve conservative former ministers, headed by Catargiu, and to see that their wealth was confiscated, on the grounds that they had squandered the country's finances. Carol was vehemently opposed, indicating that after ten years of rule he had had enough of circus shows and vendettas. But unprecedented turmoil had arisen not only to the north but also to the south of the Danube. In Bosnia and Herzegovina the Christians had risen up against the Ottoman yoke, Serbia and Montenegro had declared war on the Porte (Prince Nikola having won a few pallid victories), the uprisings in the Bulgarian lands had been smothered under the *yatağans* of the Turkish *başbuzuks*, while in Istanbul itself, at the very heart of the empire, Sultan Abdülaziz had been driven out of the Dolmabahçe Sarayı, and three months later the usurper, Murad V, had been declared insane and banished from both throne and harem. The new padishah, Abdülhamid II, his mind caught up in burning matters, such as Russia's threat to break off diplomatic relations and Great Britain's intention to convene a Balkan peace conference, closed his eyes or else paid no heed when on the banks of the Dîmbovitza, immediately after the celebration of the tenth anniversary of the enthronement of Carol I, medals with the head of the prince were cast and national decorations established, in defiance of the stipulations of the princely *firman*.

By now the railroad traversed the Balota and Severin forests, and followed the course of the Danube as far as the western frontier at Vîrciorova, by the island of Ada-Kaleh, where it linked up to the Austrian railways and the sparkle of Vienna; it made the outline of the Principalities more prominent on the maps of the continent and fulfilled one of Prince Karl Ludwig's abiding obsessions. Then, as the great city labored to cast off its Turkish raiment, all kinds of changes were made, some merely a matter of airs and graces, such as Ishlik-

Makers Street becoming French Street, others radical, involving the demolition of old buildings and construction of new ones, in particular on the sites of a number of old monasteries that had been impoverished by the nationalization of the monastic estates under Cuza. At the whim of their modish new owners, Manuc's Inn was rechristened the Hotel Dacia, the Otel Otetelşeanu became the Hôtel Frascatti, the Slătineanu Restaurant became the Capşa, after the brother confectioners, while the Church of Saint John the Great, founded by the boyar Preda Buzescu and rebuilt by Brîncoveanu, was razed to the ground with sledgehammers and pickaxes, along with its cells, stables, and outbuildings. Only the abbot's house was spared, into which was moved, after renovation, the Savings and Loans Bank. Not far away, at the eastern end of the boulevard across the road from the University, where Saint Sava Church had been reduced to a mound of rubble, there appeared a square with lanes and young trees, in one corner of which Grigore Şuţu, proprietor of the adjacent palace, built at his own personal expense hothouses with palm trees, cacti, and other never-before-seen plants, to match the pelicans, pheasants, and peacocks in his courtyard. And there, in the very center of the town, while sparse, yellowed leaves still hung from the branches of the trees, preparations were under way for the unveiling of the first statue in Bucuresci. It was November 1876, and the only sculptures people were familiar with were the stone crosses with Slavonic inscriptions that had been erected at crossroads to drive out evil spirits from the city's slum districts. And so the news of the twenty-foot-tall bronze monument was cause for general excitement. Reading the newspapers from cover to cover and sensing which way the wind was blowing, Herr Strauss had learned that it was to be an equestrian statue, fashioned by Albert Carrier de

Belleuse, in Paris, portraying one of the voievods dear to the hearts of Wallachians, Mihai the Brave. The matter did not enthuse him in the least, perhaps because he had seen hundreds of statues in his life, not only on the Unter den Linden, but also in every small German town, in the churches if not in the streets, perhaps because of the indifference that had settled over him since the deceptive audience at the palace, perhaps because in that sour season, when he had emphatically understood that he was forty years old, he preferred to play with Sănducu or to chat with his friends than to be jostled by a crowd of gawpers. And on the eighth day of the month he would undoubtedly have idled around the house if Elena had not insisted that they go out together, buy some chrysanthemums, and join the curious onlookers hurrying to cheer the prince. For almost a week, his wife had been overwhelmed by the fever of her blood and maiden name, hoping with all her heart that Prince Carol would not refrain from firm, even warlike, action, which in the roiling turmoil of the Balkans would have been a breath of fresh air for Serbia. Karl Ludwig, as they saw him from the pavement by the university, through the headscarves, hats, and caps, through the fluttering handkerchiefs and flowers, bore himself with superb confidence. As the young nation did not yet have an anthem, he flawlessly saluted during the triumphal march intoned by the brass band. Then he stepped out in front of the guard platoon, gave a short nod to the diplomats, ministers, and generals, came to a stop before the monument concealed beneath veils of white canvas, grasped the ropes handed to him, tugged them and let the soft casing tumble, like a thin layer of snow. For a good few minutes, he listened to the gasps of the crowd and let them gaze upon the mounted voievod, towering atop his stallion from a massive marble plinth, upon whose sides were emblazoned the arms of Wallachia, Moldavia, and Transylvania. And all the people saw how the Unifier, in his cast-bronze form, wore a plumed cap, held the reins in his right hand and an axe aloft in his left, with a sheathed sword at his hip, while the tail of his slightly rearing steed was wind-blown even in the calm of that tranquil, breezeless morning. Then, in a solemn ceremony, in which Joseph detected something of the rhythm and ritual of the Potsdam officers' school, the sovereign handed new, sanctified battle flags to the thirty-two regiments of the army. In a kind of exaltation, the former Miss Duković deciphered the motto embroidered on the flags in gold thread, *For honor and homeland,* and later she clapped wildly, when, by chance, a snatch of the prince's speech reached her ears: *"I am convinced that the time for courage has not passed . . ."*

As he left the square, with his horse bridled to a walk, Karl Ludwig gave a start. Among the thousands of faces, his eyes had met the eyes of Joseph Strauss. They were still hazel. He smiled at him and, looking at the woman pressed to his shoulder, he raised his hand to the peak of his cap.

Joseph and the prince did not speak until one year after that occasion, one year and three days, to be exact, when the darkness stretched like black water over the hills around Plevna, interrupted only by dwindling fires kindled from thistles, tree stumps, and cornstalks. Perhaps even then they would not have managed to talk at leisure, the two of them alone, if the prince, in his general's uniform and accompanied by a few adjutants, had not entered that afternoon the large, flimsy tent that served as a field hospital. Treading among the stretchers huddled on the ground, in the reek of blood, guts, and putrid puttees, beneath the groans and screams of the wounded, he espied the dentist at one of the operating tables, his shirtsleeves rolled up, that very dentist who had been so knowledgeable about enchanted teas. And the dentist, now busy with anything but incisors, molars, and canines, was at that moment pouring half a bottle of plum brandy down the throat of a wan infantryman, whose right leg, shattered by shrapnel from a shell, was oozing pus and had turned as yellow as a honeycomb. The dentist wiped his face with a towel, asked the orderlies to tie down the terrified soldier, raised the bottle to his own lips and took a slug, selected a hacksaw, and by the light of a sputtering lamp began to cut above the knee, well above, almost below the hip. Leaning against a wooden post, watching, Carol heard, in the brief pauses between the howls, how the canvas of the tent whooshed in the wind. He grew dizzy, and, emerging for air, thought the whooshing was like the swift wing beats of a flock of wild ducks. In the sleet outside, not seventeen hours since the slaughter around Rahova, he lit a cigar, the hundredth, and pretended not to notice the colonel behind him, who was doubled up and clutching his stomach. He let him throw up undisturbed near a wild rose bush. He gazed up at the gray clouds, the crescent moon flags on the ramparts, the rows of trenches mired in mud, the slumbering cannons, and the shivering outlines of the horses. He heard whoops and the strains of an accordion coming from the Russian positions (and he knew that they had just shared out the vodka ration), and he shuffled his damp feet and thanked God that they were still there, in their boots. He felt the glow of his cigar warming him; he smoked and waited for the amputation in the tent to be finished. And when it was over, Herr Strauss appeared, wearing a crumpled tunic, with the epaulettes of a major, and a crooked belt. His cheeks were pallid, unshaven for a week, there were blue circles under his eyes, and his hair was disheveled. He tried to salute, but when his fingers reached his temples, he realized that he was not wearing his cap and so refrained. He looked at the prince in a strange way, as though he both did and did not see him, and his eyes were as misty as the dusk. He was quick to answer all the prince's questions, not in German but in Romanian, but he avoided details and intimacies. He said *no* when the matter of a fine powder, good for infusions and delight, came up, he said *yes* when he was invited to take a glass of cognac at a quarter to ten, he shrugged when he was offered an escort for the journey through the night, and, at last, as the officers in the retinue were getting ready to mount, he, too, asked a question, in a hoarse voice, namely whether the prince was happy at having conquered that wretched redoubt, Rahova.

That spring, there had gathered around Joseph, like moths to a flame, countless omens and occurrences presaging war, some known to him, others of which he was not aware. Elena, for example, had toiled for days on end to cut from cloth, stitch, and stuff with scrunched-up newspaper a little Turkish infantryman, no more than three feet tall, on which she traced a mouth with rouge and a nose, eyes, and eyebrows with charcoal, a soldier whom Sănducu daily stabbed with his sword, throttled in furious wrestling bouts, used as a target for his bow and arrows, and whacked over the head with the stick used for stirring maize porridge. That same month, April 1877, the crown council had been urgently convened. The Tsar's army had received permission to use the railroad to reach the front in the Balkans. General mobilization had been decreed, and a number of regiments had marched to the Danube. Bukharest found itself overrun by Russians, who seemed more numerous, more raucous, and more clinging than flies. The sultan's cannons had managed to bombard Brăila, Calafat, Bechet, and Oltenitza. The Romanian artillery, in response, had rained cannonballs on the fortresses on the other shore. On the penultimate day of the month, after protracted vacillation, the Chamber had declared, with 58 votes for, 29 against, and 5 abstentions, a state of war against the Sublime Porte. In the madness that gripped the city, the dentist and the barber, while frequenting taverns, strolling at the fall of twilight, and drinking schnapps on the upper floor of the red-brick house, kept trying to get to the bottom of a particular question. In a period when patriotism wafted through the air along with the poplar fluff, when in churches, by crossroads, and at balls money was being raised for the troops, when volunteers were being lured with all kinds of promises, and when Princess Elisabeth herself had been caught up in the fervor, abandoning her poetry to set up a corps of nurses, Joseph Strauss and Otto Huer kept asking themselves whether they, as Germans, had done enough for the Principalities when they arranged that at the intersection of Lipscani Street and Boiangiu Lane the country's second statue should be erected, a plump nymph with bared shoulders, symbolizing commerce. The barber, who had paid very dearly indeed to avoid being called up, had felt blessed by heaven when the cream of the Russian army was billeted at the nearby Şerban Vodă inn. His shop was besieged daily, because those men, some wearing white tunics with pistachio-colored braids, many in boots as polished as glass, could not imagine letting more than a few hours elapse without tidying and pomading their mustaches, without shaving, without straightening their sideburns, without adjusting their hair to their liking. Thanks to this good fortune and the money that had fallen into his lap out of the clear blue sky, Otto had hired three apprentices and had stationed on the street, under a shady canopy, three new chairs, equipped with oval mirrors and small enameled basins. Herr Strauss might also have rejoiced in the new patients that had appeared overnight, but the easily earned rubles left him cold. He felt gloomy when he saw so many officers in his surgery with sturgeon bones embedded in their gums, with remnants of endive stuck between their teeth, and with breath sweetened by alcohol. To his mind they all bode ill, like owls. They conjured up misfortune and catastrophe. They reminded him of Elena's heavy silences, Elena who did not ask him to go off to war, but demanded it of him with her sighs. And they made him think of the army's small number of medics, a thought that gave him white hairs and forced him to acknowledge that before becoming a dentist he had been a doctor and knew how to wield a scalpel. In her silent insistence, his wife never ceased to teach him a complex science, that of love, without resorting to charts of the heavens, telescopes, or compasses, as in astronomy, but instead to the art of gazing at the floor, blinking, turning down the corners of her lips, dressing in haste and undressing in stealth, kissing him sparsely and wearily, sometimes wearing the dress he liked best, the swishing one with the low-cut neck and flounces, leaving newspapers open at the pages praising volunteers to the skies, sighing for the fate of vanquished Serbia, and humming songs about heroes while she cooked or ironed. Furthermore, one Sunday morning, under her downcast, white countenance, as white as cream in early May, Sănducu had appeared carrying the ruddy calfskin bag, and had asked Joseph to sprinkle liquors on the dead soldiers to bring them back to life. Joseph said nothing and promised nothing. He caressed the lad, took the bag, tested its weight in his palms as though on a pair of scales, examined the faint traces of the letter S, placed it on top of the wardrobe, and thought of his mother and sister. In the evening, Otto

Huer made light of the whole scene, laughing at the idea of going off to the front. But the dentist could no longer tolerate jokes, and Otto had to go home early, together with Ritza. After Prince Carol had somberly and rhythmically read the declaration of Romanian independence, on May 10th, eleven years to the day since his elevation to the throne, giving tavern keepers, against their better instincts, occasion to unstop barrels of their best wine, women to sob uncontrollably, urchins to yell and break the windows of the caravanserai, dogs to bark in chorus, and men to get dead drunk, Joseph had allowed one more Sunday to pass, and then placed himself at the disposal of Davila, the doctor and general who headed the army's medical corps. And in the middle of July, when the Russians no longer crowded into Otto Huer's barbershop, but were beyond the Danube, harried by the Ottomans and riddled with fly and mosquito bites, demanding assistance from the troops of Wallachia, the upholsterer who had once replaced the yellow velvet on the dentist's chairs in the winter of 1869 rummaged through his workshop, opened the lids of trunks, rubbed his chin, and gave his apprentices an unusual task. He made them take from the chests all the scraps of old material accumulated over a lifetime, cram them into sacks and take them to the edge of Bucuresci by cart, to the shredding machine with its presses and cutters. Soon, as a distant rumble wafted from the southern front, the psalms of Siegfried's youth, inscribed on pieces of yellow velvet, had been transformed into lint for the soldiers' wounds and were soaked with human blood.

The escort for Joseph Strauss arrived at half past nine, just as he was finishing off the stewed cabbage left over in his mess tin from lunch. He dusted himself down, smoothed his uniform, put on a large cape and set off alongside the two elite cavalrymen with rifles slung over their shoulders. They proceeded behind the trenches and earthworks and skirted the huge corral in which the cavalry horses were snuffling. The doctor thought for a moment of the blind woman and how the world must seem to her like a miry cave. They went around the back of a copse and stopped when a sentinel cried out at the top of his lungs and cocked his rifle. Then one of the cavalrymen pronounced a comical password, which sounded like the name of a fowl, and they disappeared behind a hillock and into a vineyard, out of the range of Turkish shells. At the next sentry's cry, they stood still in the cold, viscous darkness, in which not a star was visible. From a building with lights burning in the windows, surrounded by tall trees, which must have been poplars, a man with a torch emerged and approached them. It was a lieutenant, perhaps a clerk or secretary, who gave Joseph a textbook salute. The cavalrymen who had escorted him vanished in the direction of some gray outbuildings, and the two officers headed toward the small manor house. On the veranda, Major Strauss was greeted by a short infantryman without a cap, who set about cleaning his boots with the dexterity of a shoeshine boy. Once inside, in the empty hallway, he was asked to take a seat. After ten minutes, he rose to his feet, stood to attention as best he could, and studied the generals and colonels who were leaving the conference chamber. When the voices giving orders had died away and the rumble of the horses' hooves had faded into the distance, the prince appeared and invited him into another room. They sat in wicker armchairs, eight years and three months since their last meeting (or ninety-nine months, according to the dentist's reckoning). At first, they were silent, they cleaned their pipes, filled them with tobacco, lit them, looked at the bare walls, one of them coughed and the other ran his fingers through his hair, they clinked glasses, they each took a sip of cognac and rolled the warm liquid around the insides of their cheeks, and then the prince, as always before, poured out the things that were most on his mind: he told of troop movements plotted on charts by the general staff, hinting at the vanities and rivalries of the high-ranking officers, he spoke of morale, placing soldiers, horses, and cannons on an equal footing, each with their own requirements, for warm clothes and cartridges, for horseshoes and fodder, for cannonballs and gunpowder, he showed concern about the impending winter and the patience of Osman Pasha, who tolerated the interminable siege and would not emerge to counterattack, he alluded to his old dreams with regard to independence, trains, and a dynasty, and at this point, Joseph suddenly interrupted him and began describing his son, Alexandru. It seemed pointless to him to bring up the other son, Petre. His hazel eyes looked deeply into the blue eyes of Karl Ludwig, but he found only puzzlement and new dreams, nothing of the shadows of the past. It was midnight when the prince, sitting by the warm stove, unbuttoned his tunic and felt the need to take off his boots. He rang a little bell and the short infantryman entered with a basin in his left hand, a jug of hot water in his right, and a towel over his shoulder. He carefully pulled off his master's boots, removed the damp socks, rolled up his trouser legs, and washed his feet, soaping them twice. Then he brought some checked slippers, bowed, and left with the boots under his arm, ready to grease and buff them, for they would have to be worn again at dawn by the sleepless man with the bushy beard, the commander of all the Romanian and Russian regiments that encircled Plevna. Carol poured more brandy, stretched out in his armchair, and, his hands interlocked behind his neck, he enquired whether the reserves of lint and bandages were sufficient, whether he, Joseph, could bear to see so many men maimed and dying, whether he managed to sleep, and whether he thought that the Turks' tasseled fezzes brought them luck, in addition to their bellicosity, their stratagems, the logic of battles, and the seasons. At last, after much gloomy talk, the prince yawned deeply, and Herr Strauss made a single request. He wanted a letter to arrive in Bucuresci, without fail, at number 18, Lipscani Street, not like the letters before it, which had been scattered to the winds.

On parting, noticing that a frost had settled, the doctor looked at his pocket watch with the gilded lid and saw that it was five to three. He peered at the plains, he had an inkling that the dawn, not long thence, would be bloody in the major assault, he melted with yearning, imagining Elena's face on the pillow, and her body hidden beneath the sheets, he knew that neither Karl Ludwig nor anyone else would ever find out that the prince was Petre's father, he remembered the first love-choked lines of his letter and he thought of everything he had asked for from home, most of all, at that moment in the depths of the night, woolen socks and coffee. Near the tent, he saw a fox rooting in the ash where a fire had been burning. It was lame and frightened.

Now that he was living alone with the tomcat once more, Joseph had given up the pipes that had consumed his time and nerves, and switched to cigarettes, smoking three times as much. He coughed in the mornings, always waking Siegfried, he would heat some water, wash, shave, and however the light of the new day shone and however much he wanted to forget, looking in the mirror as the razor glided over his cheeks he remembered Elena's shrieks, her tears, her blazing eyes, and her devastating fury during which she had smashed windows and plates, torn paintings from the walls and trampled them underfoot, slashed curtains, sheets, and drapes, screaming continually and cursing him for lying to her his whole life, for cheating on her and humiliating her, for having a blind mistress and a bastard child, kept hidden away and provided for. As a rule, while he revisited the devastating crisis and heard again the explosions and curses, the tomcat would sit by the washstand, on his hind paws, with his tail raised and his black ear pricked up, studying him. They moved together when the dentist placed the coffeepot and the pan in which he fried eggs, ham, or slices of ewe's cheese on the hob. Again, Siegfried would be waiting when they sat down at the table to chew in silence. They would both gaze at the alpine landscape, which hung on the nail Elena had hammered into her chosen place, a painting that now had two large holes, one in the middle and one in the lower left corner, made by her shoe heels. Sometimes, at night, when he could not sleep, the painting haunted Joseph, though his eyes no longer saw it, because in the larder he had found a flacon wrapped in cloth, placed in a sealed jar, a jar hidden in a box tied up with string, behind other boxes, sacks of lentils, flour, coarse sugar, buckwheat, beans, pearl barley, and rice. And therein was the powdered *Amanita muscaria,* which had lost none of its potency. It was not until October 1880, eight months after her departure, amid thunderclaps and bolts of lightning, when valises, chests, and bundles had tumbled down the stairs, when Sănducu had been thrust from behind like a stubborn foal, when the blue Serbian eyes had flashed like the blade of a dagger and her threats had whizzed like bullets, that Herr Strauss discovered a crack in the iciness with which his wife now treated him. She had sent him news, via a servant of Baron Nikolić of Rudna, that she would receive him once every four weeks in the small wing of the house in the Udricani quarter, so that he might see the boy. And during a snowstorm, on his third visit, shortly before the German Christmas, he had permitted himself to ask for a cup of hot tea, taking advantage of the fact that she had thanked him for the presents in the child's stead. Sănducu, who was now more than ten and a half, was out sledding on a bank above Saint Venera Church and was supposed to return soon. While Elena was boiling the water in the servants' kitchen, Joseph remained alone in the room, in an armchair with a rounded back. He was sitting cross-legged, his head resting on his right hand. He wanted to smoke, but he touched neither tobacco tin nor matches. And because since the war he had been left not only with nightmares but also a weapon, he felt his chest pocket, over his heart, to convince himself that the pistol was inside. As he waited for the tea, which seemed to be taking an eternity, he watched a large, groggy fly, brought back to life by the warmth of the candle on the nightstand. He took out the pistol, and passing it from one hand to the other, he thought of the answer he had given, the only answer he had been able to give that furious and unforgiving woman; he repeated it in his mind five or six times, *It isn't true!* He opened the chamber, saw the bullet inside, closed it, and spun it as hard as he could. After all, he had fought for more than a year alongside Russians and learned what they meant by *roulette*. Finally, he closed his eyes, pressed the barrel of the pistol to his forehead, and squeezed the trigger. He heard nothing but a soft, brief metallic click. When Elena entered with a tray on which there were three steaming teacups and a sugar bowl, the dentist was bathed in sweat. He wiped his forehead with a handkerchief and sipped his tea, taking care not to scald himself. It was good. Lime tea. From all the cigarettes, his chest felt like a rickety stovepipe, full of soot and spiderwebs.

8 ❖ The Parade

AND WHEN THE TENTH of May came around yet again, in the year 1881, unparalleled festivities commenced, celebrations at which the now gray-haired Prince Carol, after bringing the country tranquility, trains, statues, a resounding military victory, street lamps, independence, a new province (Dobrudja), a Western breeze, and cigarettes instead of hookahs, was to be crowned king. At dawn, Bucuresci awoke to a twenty-one-cannon salute, and a little after one, when the royal cortege had long since covered the distance from the Tîrgoviște Station to the Metropolia and after the lengthy service to consecrate the crowns had come to a close, the city once more quaked, this time to the sound of one hundred cannons, for the peace of the souls in Heaven, for long life to the monarchs, and for the joy of that crowd, awash in cheers, flowers, tricolor flags, and more cheers. The royal coach, drawn by eight white horses, then crossed the Dîmbovitza, slowly advanced down Podul Mogoșoaiei, flanked by squadrons of cavalrymen and lancers, and came to a stop in front of the palace, once more allowing the throng to marvel at the crown, fashioned from the steel of a Turkish cannon captured at Plevna.

The festivities continued in the throne room, from where, since there still was no Romanian anthem, the strains of "Got erhalte," the Austrian anthem, resounded as far as the surrounding lanes. Four thousand envoys from towns and villages laid large bouquets on the podium, until it seemed that not only all the lilies, roses, and peonies of Romania had been heaped there, but those of an entire continent.

Reading Goethe for the fifth time and knowing all too well that Faust's Margarete had not one drop of Serbian blood, Joseph Strauss refused to take part in the commotion on the streets — the cannons, uniforms, and battle flags would have reminded him of the war and of the brilliance of Karl Ludwig. He chose instead to watch the parade of allegorical floats the next day, hoping that it would be a calmer spectacle. And on the morning of May 11, he found himself in the front row of onlookers, with the wicker basket hanging from his arm, its lid raised, so that Siegfried, now seventeen years of age, old and frail as he was, might still taste something of life's pleasures. Beside him stood Petre, whose hair would not stay combed flat and whose mustache had begun to sprout. Won over, they watched together the slow procession of those stage sets on wheels, drawn by dozens of oxen and young horses, bearing rich, carefully crafted tableaux, each outdoing the last in its resplendence of color, abundance of gilded stucco statuettes and ornamentation, perfection of detail, length of velvet, satin, and silk, and the artistry of its protagonists' gestures and movements, as they moved toward the viewing stand where Karl Ludwig and Elisabeth Pauline were sitting, enchanted. In the slow parade, the float of the jewelers, watchmakers, and silversmiths had just passed, followed by the float of the masons, carpenters, and painters, which represented an ancient city, with a priestess atop each tower and a temple to the goddess Juno rising above the ramparts. Violins, *cobza*s, and zithers resounded from the float of the gypsy musicians and flower sellers, and then came the floats of the hatters, tailors, cobblers, quilt makers, upholsterers, and many more. As the float of the confectioners and pastry makers was passing, and Joseph was gazing in wonder at the gigantic cake, with its multifarious crèmes melting in the sun, Siegfried jumped out of the basket, mewed at the top of his lungs, and shot across the road. He was not as agile as he had been, and he slipped in the splashes of liquefied butter and landed under the hooves of a horse. He let out a terrible howl and then lay limp on the cobbles, much to the amusement of the crowd. Crying out something in German, the dentist broke through the line of gendarmes and ran over to the tomcat. However, from the other side of the road, a woman with a sun hat and tiny boots, like a doll's, had already burst through the crowd, lifted Siegfried up, and was clutching him to her breast. It was Elena Strauss. Behind her stood Sănducu. He was pale and trembling. Together they moved away from the route of the parade, without hearing the whoops and whistles around them, they emerged from the throng, and stopped under a chestnut tree. The tomcat's mouth was lolling open. He was barely breathing and twitched from time to time. As their damp cheeks glistened, Elena noticed the other boy. He was older than her own, and he had a slightly hooked nose, bushy eyebrows, beveled cheekbones, and a cleft in the middle of his chin. She turned her head, looking now into the distance at the royal podium where Carol was standing, now at Petre's face, as if trying to make out something through the trees, beyond the allegorical floats and the tops of thousands of heads.

With the cat in her arms, she was unable to embrace Joseph, but she pressed up against him and covered his cheeks, eyelids, and lips with kisses. And there, in the shade, as the days of Siegfried the tomcat came to a close, the days of the King were about to begin.

Notes

Political Background

The Ottoman Empire

When *The Days of the King* begins, in 1866, the two principalities, Moldavia and Wallachia, which in 1918 were unified with Transylvania, Bukowina, the Banat and Maramureş (provinces formerly part of the Austro-Hungarian Empire) and Bessarabia (part of the Russian Empire after 1812) to become Greater Romania, were under the suzerainty of the Ottoman Empire, referred to in the book from time to time as the "Sublime Porte." The term "Sublime Porte" is a synecdoche for the Empire (as we might say "London" or "Washington" for England or the United States) and it originally referred to the gate of the headquarters of the Grand Vizier in the Topkapı Palace in Istanbul, where the sultan held the greeting ceremony for foreign ambassadors. The Ottoman Empire, which had been in existence since the thirteenth century, was declining in political and military power. But its capital city remained a site of architectural splendor, especially the Dolmabahçe Sarayı, the sultan's palace, built between 1843 and 1856. Some other Turkish vocabulary that may be useful: a "firman" was a royal mandate or decree; a "hatti-şerif" was, similarly, an edict; a "yatağan" is a type of Turkish sword; and the "başbuzuks" were irregular soldiers of the Ottoman Army.

Moldavia and Wallachia were not part of the territory of the Ottoman Empire per se, but rather vassal states, required to pay a yearly tribute; the Turks also exerted a strong influence on the succession or election of the local Moldavian and Wallachian rulers. In 1857, councils of citizens of the two principalities convened to discuss their political future. These councils were called the "ad hoc Divans" ("divan" being the Ottoman term for "council"), and they concluded that the two principalities wanted unification under hereditary rule by a foreign prince. *The Days of the King* begins just after the abdication of Alexander John Cuza, a Moldavian nobleman and politician who had served as the *Domnitor* ("lord" or "ruler") of the United Principalities from 1859 until 1866, in lieu of an acceptable, available foreign prince.

Moldavia and Wallachia were not alone in their movement towards independence: most of the Balkan countries were also either tributaries or part of the Empire, and their independence struggles are referred to in the novel in the mention of "Bulgarian insurgents" on page 124 and uprisings in Bosnia, Herzegovina, Serbia, Montenegro, and Bulgaria on page 179.

Romanian Politics

All of the Romanian politicians referred to in the book are real historical figures and many of them were very influential

in the course of Romanian history: the *Golescu* family pro-
duced three prime ministers, *Nicolae, Ştefan, and Alexandru;*
Dinicu Golescu, the father of the three, was a noted man of
letters.

Like the Golescus, the Ghikas were an old boyar family; boyars were a class of landed nobility that had emerged
from chiefs of rural communities in the early Middle Ages.
Ion Ghika and *Dimitrie Ghika* both served as Prime Minister under Carol I, though for opposite parties (Liberal
and Conservative, respectively). Ion Ghika's position as bey
of Samos is mentioned several times: the island of Samos,
like the rest of Greece, was an Ottoman possession and Ion
Ghika was appointed "bey" or governor of the island in 1854.
He served with distinction for five years, succeeding especially in combating piracy during the Crimean War, and became adept and knowledgeable in Ottoman political manu-
vering. In 1859, he was called to the United Principalities by
the newly elected Cuza and took up the post of prime minister. He served in the same position under Carol I. In 1870–71,
however, he was part of the anti-monarchical movement that
erupted with the "Ploesci Republic." Dimitrie Ghika's nickname, Beyzade Mitică, mentioned at one point in the book,
needs a little explanation: "Mitică" is a diminutive for "Dimitrie" and "beyzade" means "son of a bey."

Lascar Catargiu was a member, like Nicolae Golescu, of
the Princely Lieutenancy, a ruling triumvirate established after the forced abdication of Cuza on February 11, 1866. In the
Lieutenancy, Catargiu represented Moldavia and the conservatives, Golescu Wallachia and the liberals, and Nicolae Hara-
lambie the Army. In May 1866, after the ascension of Carol I
to the throne, Catargiu became prime minister, but unable to

work with liberals Ion C. Brătianu and C. A. Rosetti he resigned in July. He later held various ministerial posts and, after the period of anti-monarchical agitation in 1870–71, formed Romania's first stable conservative cabinet, which lasted until 1876.

Ion C. Brătianu (nicknamed the Vizier), who appears many times in the novel, played a major role in the politics of Carol's era and founded a political dynasty that lasted well into the twentieth century. Brătianu, from a wealthy Wallachian family, was an advocate of the Moldavian and Wallachian union, and independence from the Ottomans, from the 1840s onwards. He served in Cuza's government as a leader of the Liberal party and was instrumental in the ousting of Cuza and the choice of Karl Ludwig. Under Carol, he held a number of offices, including minister of war. He had a stormy and complicated political career, including involvement in the Ploesci rebellion of 1870, but would eventually preside as Prime Minister over the longest stable government in Romanian history, 1876–1888.

The historical precedent for a unified Romania made up of Moldavia, Wallachia, and Transylvania was set by *Mihai (or Michael) the Brave* in 1600. A Wallachian prince, Mihai conquered Moldavia and Transylvania, and ruled all three for a short period. His victory was soon overturned, and Mihai had no nationalistic project, but he became the symbol of Romanian unification in the nineteenth century. Mihai is referred to as a "voievod," a Slavic title denoting the commander of a military force. *Stephen the Great,* also mentioned, was Prince of Moldavia in the late fifteenth century. Powerful, victorious in many battles, and pious, he is a hero of Romanian history and represents Moldavian glory.

Military Background

The years that *The Days of the King* is set in, 1866 to 1881, were years of frequent military conflicts across the European continent, as the most powerful states—Austria, Prussia, France, Great Britain, Russia, the Ottoman Empire—jockeyed for control over territory and systems of government. The first war mentioned in the book, the one that is beginning just as Joseph Strauss leaves Berlin, is the **Austro-Prussian War,** fought from the middle of June through late August of 1866. (Switzerland is neutral during this war, which is why Joseph originally travels to Switzerland for a Swiss passport; with a Prussian passport, he would not have been able to pass through Austria into the United Principalities.) The opposing sides were Prussia, led by Prime Minister Otto von Bismarck, and its ally Italy, and Austria, along with its allies, a number of the German states including Bavaria, Saxony, and Hanover. It resulted in a decisive Prussian victory after the battle of Sadowa/Königgrätz in East Bohemia. This is also the war in which Prince Karl's younger brother, Anton von Hohenzollern, is wounded and dies, after encountering the Crown Prince of Prussia himself on the battlefield.

The war that is the cause of anti-German sentiment in Bucharest and the attack on Lipscani Street (page 152) is the **Franco-Prussian War** (1870–1871). The combatants were Prussia, led by King Wilhelm I and Bismarck, and France, led by Napoleon III. The war was fought primarily on the border between the two countries; it ended in French defeat and the surrender of Napoleon at the battle of Sedan in northern France. In the United Principalities, a strong tradition of Francophilia influenced public opinion about the war. From approximately the 1830s onwards, there had been great admiration for and a sense of affiliation with all things French, political, cultural, linguistic, and otherwise. Indeed, in the founding myths of Romania as a modern nation state, France is the "older Latin sister" and Romania an "island of Latinity" in a "sea of Slavs."

The war that Joseph Strauss eventually enlists in as a medic is the **Russo-Turkish War** of 1877–1878. The conflict began in 1875 with anti-Ottoman uprisings in Bosnia, Herzegovina, and then Bulgaria. The uprising in Bulgaria in particular was brutally crushed by the Ottomans with the use of *başbuzuks*. In short order, Serbia declared war on the Ottoman Empire, and was soon militarily overwhelmed. Then Russia followed suit and declared war on the Empire, ostensibly on behalf of the Bulgarians (who were Orthodox Christians) but also to restore Russian influence in the region, which had been much reduced after Russia's defeat in the Crimean War. In Plevna, a town in northern Bulgaria, the Ottomans dug in and were besieged by the Russian Army which initially suffered heavy losses. They appealed to the Romanians for reinforcements and Carol I agreed, on the condition that he would be in charge of both armies. Shortly after signing a treaty with the Russians, allowing them to pass through Romanian territory, the Romanians formally declared their independence from the Ottoman Empire in May 1877. The Russian-Romanian coalition defeated the Ottomans and the northern Bulgarian province of Dobrudja was given in tribute to Romania.

Religious Background

The predominant faith in Romania at the time this book is set was Eastern Orthodox Christianity, and the largest and most imposing church in Bucharest was the Cathedral of the Metropolia, presided over by His Beatitude Metropolitan Nifon. Born Nicolae Rusailă, he entered the brotherhood, taking the name Nifon, in 1809 at Cernica Monastery. He rose through the ecclesiastical ranks and in 1865, he became Metropolitan Primate, head of the Orthodox Church in the United Principalities. He founded an ecclesiastical printing press and using the revenues from his estate at Letca, south of Bucharest, he built and restored churches, established a seminary, and performed other charitable works.

Certain customs unique to the Eastern Orthodox Church appear in the novel, for instance, the custom of having godparents for weddings, as well as for baptisms. When Joseph and Elena are married, they have a godfather and a godmother who participate in the ceremony and whose relationship, as in a baptism, is not confined merely to the event; the godparents become spiritual parents to the couple thereafter.

Eastern Orthodox Christianity does not, in the religiously open Bucharest of the time, mean only the Romanian Orthodox Church: Elena belongs to the Serbian Orthodox Church, which has its own national and local saints, though the major feasts and the rituals are the same. The Russian brothers from the Visarion quarter whom Otto Huer recommends to Joseph Strauss are "Old Believers," a sect that broke from the central church in the seventeenth century, protesting the liturgical reforms of Patriarch Nikon in 1652. They adhered to older forms of prayer, forbid the shaving of beards, and practiced an ascetic lifestyle. The brothers are referred to as "Filippovian" (Russian *Filippovetsy*), indicating that they are members of the group of Old Believers who emigrated from Russia to escape persecution under Peter the Great and settled in the Danube Delta.

When Joseph Strauss and Peter Bykow go rabbit-hunting in the countryside, near Bulgaria, they encounter a co-religionist of theirs, a Catholic priest, Necula Penov, who addresses them in Slavonic and Latin. Old Church Slavonic is in fact a dialect of Old Bulgarian that was used as a literary and liturgical language from the ninth century; thus like Latin, used by the Roman Catholic Church, it was not a "living" language; of course, Old Church Slavonic would have been more intelligible to ordinary Bulgarians than it was to Romanians. Bulgaria was an Orthodox nation; Catholics like Penov were therefore schismatics, outcasts, forced to make a life for themselves in obscurity, in strong contrast to the religious freedom experienced by Joseph and Peter in Bucharest.

Another form of faith altogether is represented in the mention of the Blazhini (page 88). In Romanian and Balkan folklore, the *Blazhini* (literally "gentle" or "meek ones"; Romanian *Blajini*) are descended from Seth, the son of Adam. The *Blazhini* live at the ends of the earth, they wear no clothes and eat nothing but the fruits they find growing in the wilderness. The men and women live apart and meet only once a year in order to have children. The source of the legend was probably travelers' tales about the gymnosophists of India. The River at the Ends of the Earth is called in Romanian Sîmbăta, literally Saturday (the word is from Old Slavonic *Sǫbota,* cf. Russian *Subbota,* ultimately from Hebrew *shabat*). "A se duce pe apa Sîmbetei" (to go down the waters of the Saturday) means "to perish." At Easter, it was the custom to cast the shells of Easter eggs onto flowing waters so that they would float away to the ends of the earth and bear the tidings of the Resurrection to the *Blazhini.*

Bucharest Background

The Days of the King immerses a reader in nineteenth-century Bucharest. A word on spelling: Bucharest is referred to in a number of different spellings to reflect the multilingual character of the city, the different states it was part of, and the novel's diverse characters. Sometimes the city is referred to as Bucuresci, which is the nineteenth-century Romanian spelling of what is now București, sometimes as Bükreș, its Ottoman Turkish name. Bukarest is the German and Yiddish spelling; also mentioned is the Russian Bukharest/Бухарест. (Note also that up until the reign of Cuza, Romanian, uniquely for a Romance language, was written using a Cyrillic alphabet adapted from Old Church Slavonic script. The Latin alphabet was introduced officially in 1860.)

Bucharest's main street, **Podul Mogoşoaiei,** now called Calea Victoriei, appears many times in the novel, especially during the courtship of Joseph and Elena. Long the main throughfare and most fashionable street in Bucharest, Podul (so-called because it was paved or floored (*podit*) with oak beams) Mogoşoaiei was created in 1692, during the reign of Constantine Brîncoveanu, Prince of Wallachia. The road led from Constantine's palace in Bucharest to his estate at Mogoşoaia, a village outside the city.

In Joseph and Elena's walks along Podul Mogoşoaiei, they pass many institutions of nineteenth-century Bucharest life: shops, theaters, clubs, hotels. A particular feature of Bucharest, and part of its Turkish inheritance, were the inns, like the Zlătari, the Kretzulescu, and the Şerban Vodă. The inns were large buildings with four wings arranged around a courtyard, with merchants' shops on the ground floor and rooms for travelers on the upper floor. Some of the inns were owned by and provided revenues for a church or monastery. An example of this is the Stavropoleos Inn (pp. 87, 110), which was connected to the Stavropoleos Monastery and its exquisitely beautiful church. There is a similar interconnectedness between districts of the city, churches, and trades: the various districts (Udricani, Brezoianu, Calicilor, Visarion, Batiştei, Silvestru, among others) were each associated with a church and were home to different trades, as the Scaune quarter is identified in the novel with butchers (cf. the passage on pages 56–57 when Joseph hears all the bells of the quarters' churches ringing).

In terms of important bodies of water, there is the **Dîmbovitza** and the **Bucureştioara**. The Dîmbovitza River is a branch of the River Argeş, itself a tributary of the Danube. During the time of the novel it supplied most of the city's drinking water, distributed by water carriers. The Bucureştioara (a diminutive of "Bucureşti"), a tributary of the Dîmbovitza, was a stream that flowed through the Scaune district. Its water was used by the butchers who plied their trade there. And there is also **Cişmigiu Park:** Cişmigiu is the oldest public park in central Bucharest and was laid out between 1847 and 1854 by Viennese landscape gardener Wilhelm Mayer on the site of what had been an area of insalubrious marshes surrounding a small lake, called the Lake of Dura the Merchant. The name derives from the Turkish *çeşmeği*, the title of Bucharest's director of public drinking fountains (Turkish *çeşme*, Romanian *cişmea*—drinking fountain), who used to live on the shore of the lake.

Significant public buildings in the book include the **Colţei Tower** and two train stations, **Filaret Station** and **Tîrgovişte Station.** The **Colţei Tower** was built in the eighteenth century as a watchtower against fires and military invasions; for a long time the tallest structure in the city, it was taken down in the 1880s. Filaret was the Bishop and later Metropolitan of the region of Rîmnic in the late eighteenth century. On the hill named after him in Bucharest there was a white marble fountain in the Turkish style, and it became a favorite spot for promenades. In time, the fountain fell into disrepair, and was demolished in 1863. Bucharest's first railway station was built on Filaret Hill in 1869. The building survives, but is now used as a bus station. The Tîrgovişte Station, now called Gara de Nord, is Bucharest's largest railway station. The foundations were laid by Carol I on September 10, 1868, and the station was inaugurated September 13, 1872, serving the Roman-Galatzi-Bucharest-Piteşti line.

And some locations outside of Bucharest: **Sinaia Monastery,** where the royal family spends summer vacations, dates from the seventeenth century. It was founded by Prince Mihail Cantacuzino after a pilgrimage to the Monastery of St. Catherine on Mount Sinai, whence the name. It is situated in the Prahova Valley, in the southern Carpathians. It was in this picturesque, alpine setting that Carol chose to build Castle Peleş.

Cotroceni is a hill and district in western Bucharest. Şerban Cantacuzino, Prince of Wallachia between 1678 and 1688, founded a monastery on Cotroceni Hill in 1679. Cuza converted the monastery into a summer residence, which was also used by King Carol I, as the wooded Cotroceni Hill provided a place of refuge from the torrid heat of Bucharest in the summer months. In 1888, King Carol I had the old monastery buildings demolished and commissioned French architect Paul Gottereau to design a palace, which nowadays is the official residence of the President of Romania.